Jon Ransom's second novel, *The Gallopers* will be published in 2024. He lives in Cambridge, UK.

'A powerful new voice of gay working-class life ... This eloquent heartfelt debut pulls the reader right beside him, and announces Ransom as a writer of real talent.' *Guardian*

'An authentic portrait of gay love in small-town Britain ... Remarkable for its atmosphere, it's arresting use of language and the way the environment serves as an extension of Joe's psyche. A potent tale.' *The Spectator*

'If you only read one debut novel this year, make it this one. *The Whale Tattoo* is a book of visceral, magnetic raw pulsating beauty. A mesmeric, gritty tour de force. We haven't read a novel this brilliant since *Swimming in the Dark* by Tomasz Jedrowski. This book is the reason that people love to read.' Uli Lenart, *Attitude Magazine*

'There are far too few books of working-class gay life, and few celebrate the emotional depth of Queer lads like *The Whale Tattoo* ... a magical exploration of grief and love.' *G Scene*

'A gripping read, unpredictable but emotionally coherent ... a surprisingly enjoyable and cathartic read.' *Queer Review*

'Ransom's writing is visceral and bold filled with lusty sex and explicit language. A brilliant evocative and unfaltering debut.' *Bookstoker*

'I can strongly recommend *The Whale Tattoo* by debutant Jon Ransom ... I cannot recall when a book – especially one from a first-time author – has had such an effect on me.' Rob Harkavy, *Out News Global*

'*The Whale Tattoo* is a stunning achievement – one of the most impressive and assured debuts I've ever read.' Matt Cain

'Raw, uncompromising, and authentic, a remarkable debut from an astonishingly gifted writer.' Golnoosh Nour

'An astonishing book. Jon Ransom's writing manages to be simultaneously brutal and violent as well as poetic and moving. The quality of his prose if mesmerising.' Linda Hill, Linda's Book Bag

'This guy is an incredible new talent. A short book that punches well above its weight: explicit, brutal and moving.' Isabel Costello, *The Literary Sofa*

'An astounding debut by an important new voice in queer literature with a completely unique sense of language. Simply a triumph' 5 ★★★★★.' *Love Reading*, Thomas Schwentenwien

'The novel scratches an itch that few books can reach. It's Ransom's raw reflection on life, his recognition of the brutality that transforms moments of passing rapture into something dreamy that leaves the reader entranced.' Neil Czeszejko, Most Anticipated Books of 2022, *Delphic Reviews*

THE WHALE TATTOO

Jon Ransom

**MUSWELL
PRESS**

First published by Muswell Press in 2022
This edition published 2023

Copyright © Jon Ransom 2022

Typeset in Bembo by M Rules
Printed and bound by
CPI Group (UK) Ltd, Croydon CR0 4YY.

Jon Ransom has asserted his right to be
identified as the author of this work in accordance
with the Copyright, Designs and Patents Act, 1988

A CIP catalogue record for this book is
available from the British Library

ISBN: 9781739879495
eISBN 9781838340124

Muswell Press
London N6 5HQ
www.muswell-press.co.uk

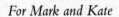

For Mark and Kate

Death has followed me here and I can prove it, because whenever something really fucked up is about to happen, my balls ache. Proof is funny like that. I've not come far. From there to here is maybe fifteen miles, but here I am watching the fairground lorries bound past, yanked out of town by a cruel wind, trusting my bollocks over the Amazing Esmeralda and her crystal ball. The tail of the convoy is all blue shiny paint and tightly folded metal, looking like the lopsided dead whale. Seems like the whale has followed me here, too. If a gigantic blue beast comes to tell you something terrible, you better pay attention. When it happens twice, believe it.

I'm sucking the smoke from my cigarette, cupping my hand to keep the rain off. What will I tell him? Birdee'd say I should keep my mouth shut, let trouble do what it does best and put my back towards it. But it's Fysh. I toss the dog-end on the ground.

With Lynn docks behind me, cranes tangled up in rows of black clouds rolling in from the east, I'm nearing the Fisher

Fleet. Here the mucky water threatens the quay at full tide. The trawlers are coming home from the Outer Roads. Gulls gliding this way and that remind me of paper aeroplanes.

I've claimed a spot beneath the brick shelter, wishing I'd found someplace to piss. On my right, the river cuts a mean line through the land. The quay is filling up with rusty trawlers heavy with shellfish. When I spot the *Ann Marie*, my stomach gets tight. Two years away is a long stretch. And then he's there, red hair like a hot match. The same stubborn way he stands. I move out from beneath the tin roof onto the quay. 'Fysh—' I shout.

Up close, he stinks of tide mud and engine oil. 'Jesus fucking Christ, mate,' he says. There's all kinds of trouble in his eyes. Hypnotising.

'Alright?'

'What the hell you doing here?' Hugging me hard.

Because I don't know where to begin, I shrug. How'd I tell him I've come home to figure out why death chases after me? We stand taking each other in, smoking a shared cigarette.

'Come on.' And I follow him until ahead of us there's nothing but the river steadily pounding the bank.

'Jesus,' he says. 'You wanna come over later?'

'Alright,' I say, and it's like I never left. The last two years just disappears. But there's more to this than the ache in my underpants. The river speaks to me.

My urgency to piss is everything, bigger than the warm mattress and the redheaded man asleep alongside me. Quietly I get up, walk the floor, look back and listen for sleep sounds. In the dim bathroom I piss into the bowl, on top of last night's urine, and flush. I pull on crunched-up jeans first because I don't know where my underpants are. My coat is still damp from yesterday's rain.

The view from the concrete balcony is nothing much to see. Clouds hang like dirty curtains. I suck in cold air, and consider the man whose bed I slept in. Fysh is dangerous. One night gone, and already he's busted beneath my skin, messing me up. And I want him inside me. Because with Fysh, there's the in-between place I go. Where there's no noise, and nothing matters. And I like it. But it's wrong. Last night, bare-arsed on his bed, I listen to him talk about how right it feels, and I tell him, 'These things you want can't ever be right.'

Fysh won't hear me. Tugs down his green underpants and tells me, 'You're wrong, mate.'

A scrawny boy riding a beaten-up-bike pedals by slowly on the pavement beneath. He calls up for a cigarette. I tell him to sod off and flick the dog-end off the balcony. Inside there's no paper and pen to leave Fysh a note. No use chewing my nails over it. Instead, I write *Joe* in ketchup on the white kitchen table, so he knows I'm not a ghost. Then I carry Birdee's pushbike down three flights of concrete steps because the lift is ruined, and ride home to the river.

With sky everywhere, the river chases alongside the track, following the line. I slow down at Black Barn, a dead place at this time of year. Rumour reckons a local buried a man beneath the dirt floor. Fysh spent one summer way back trying to prove it. Found nothing but a fistful of blisters.

Half a mile further, pushed aside by the river, is the house at the Point. It appears empty. I detour, ride by, but the worn rubber tyres are useless on wet marshland. I abandon the pushbike and finish the distance on foot. The filthy brown river licks the mudflats like a thirsty animal, the wrecked fishing trawler the only proof man has been to this place. I stoop inside, just to be sure. The hull stinks of tidal mud and rot. The half-light gives up torn planks and beaten iron. I stay long enough to run my finger over our initials carved into the wood.

Through the back door, and the radio says I've missed breakfast. Birdee is sitting at the kitchen table, rolling her hair around her finger. I peel out of my coat and hang it on the back of the kitchen chair.

'You're an idiot,' she says. 'You trying to kill yourself?'

Bare-chested, I rub at my pale skin until my fist has made a red circle in between my nipples. I open the washing machine, pull out yesterday's t-shirt, and slip it on.

'Where've you been?'

'With Fysh.' I don't care if she can smell him on me.

'Stay away from him—'

'Alright,' I say, closing my eyes and letting the silent gap sit there. My sister's been boiling me about Tim Fysh for ever.

Because I don't want to wind up Birdee, when Fysh calls later I tell her it was some twat selling something. She knows I'm a liar. Down the telephone his voice is different, words spread apart, like he's talking in tongues. Makes me anxious.

4

He says, 'Pick you up at eight, mate.' Then I'm standing in the kitchen with the telephone pressed against my ear, listening to nothing.

There's nothing much to do. Birdee's gone out to see the one-armed Soldier. He's fucked up. She's left me a bowl in the fridge. Because I'm hungry, I take her effort upstairs to the bathroom, run the taps while I sit on the toilet seat, and eat peach jelly.

In the bath I smoke three cigarettes in a row, listening to the tap drip-dripping. Sometimes it seems like I spend all my time wet. Or chased by the stuff. This water is lobster hot. It's impossible to tell sweat from bath water. I drop the dog-end into the toilet bowl, weigh up if I have time to make it downstairs to answer the ringing telephone. Fuck. But it could be Fysh. I'm half-hard thinking about him.

'Hello?' And I tell her my name. She's called something I don't catch, because she's talking a hundred miles an hour, telling me my old man will be discharged tomorrow morning. 'I'll be there,' I say. There goes my hard-on.

I refuse to look away. The woman has purple hair and dances like a blackbird around an empty goldfish bowl. She could be a remnant of something older, a trick conjured from a fairground tented on the edge of town in another time. Her shadow, dark as wet tar, is lagging behind under Friday-night streetlight. I want her to be an illusion. To disappear. But when she stops dead, I close the distance between us, ask, 'You alright?'

Bent in half, she lifts the glass bowl off the pavement, cocks her head. 'Fuck off.' And she steps over the river of piss Fysh has made.

'Barking, mate.' Fysh says. 'Bollocks.' He knocks at his forehead with his clenched fist, then goes back the way we came towards the Greenland, where we'd been drinking before Doug turned up. I lean onto the church railing, watching formless faces through fogged glass in the White Hart. A tall lad comes out with his short mate, winks. 'All right, fella?'

'Alright' I say. I don't recognise him. Even when I dig

around it's useless. Whoever tall lad had been, now he's no one. They clear off down the street, while the cold gets colder.

When Fysh comes back, still knocking away, he says, 'Stupid—forgot my lighter.' He loosely hangs his arm around my shoulder. 'Up for it?' His breath is thick with beer, cigarettes and trouble.

I tell him I have to pick up my old man from the hospital in the morning. He pushes his hand down the front of my trousers. Licks my cheek like a thirsty dog.

'Fuck off, already,' I say. He doesn't care about my old man. Mostly nobody does. Worn, I take Fysh home and leave him face down on the mattress. I don't even pull off his trainers. He mumbles, and it sounds like he's wounded, a soldier forgotten in a ditch. I want to lie down alongside and watch him for a time. That's fucked up.

Outside, the night sucks me in. Pavement wet and empty. At the Jewish cemetery I stop. White-knuckling the bars on the door, I take a look inside. These dirty-red brick walls guard sixteen broken headstones, chiselled with writing nobody can read.

I am younger than I am now when the showman from the Mart takes me to sin. Saw him first on the waltzers with Birdee. We pay our money and climb into the worn car-riage. Leather seat hot from the lads before us. He lowers the steel bar, winks. Says his name is Jimmy Bugg, same as on the rounding boards above the ride. Then he spins us. Fast. Birdee screaming, 'I'm gonna throw up.'

I'm still grinning when the ride ends, mesmerised by the

light. The way it slides like water when I hold out my hand, dripping through my fingers, soaking me with colour. We don't go far. Birdee is complaining about the rows of dirty glass bowls, half-filled and yellowed. 'It's not right.'

I don't care about the fish that are more orange than gold.

'I'm going home,' she says.

'Alright.' It doesn't matter because I'm watching Jimmy Bugg go around and around. He's like Jesus walking on wooden water. The planks rise and fall madly, unable to topple him. He keeps hungry eyes on me, worrying the hard-on in my underpants. Until I get back in the waltzer for another go. When he leans in to lock the bar down, his free hand reaches around the back of my head, grazing my hair with mean fingertips. He has a tattoo of the Virgin Mary on his neck. The ink is close enough to taste. Then everything gets blurred.

After the ride slows to a stop, he tells his mate to take over for a time. Lighting a joint, he weaves through the rowdy fair, every so often turning back to see if I'm still trailing him. The noise gets left behind.

I'm agitated. The kind of restlessness that reminds me I am fifteen years old. Makes me hop from one trainer to the other, looking like I'm getting ready to run. In the Jewish cemetery he is lit by the lamp post leaning over the wall, staining his skin yellow. 'This what you want?' Jimmy Bugg asks. His rough, red-knuckled hands work worn trouser buttons undone. I'm nodding. A ladder of dark tangled hair appears, then disappears beneath the waistband of his underpants. He tugs them down to his knees, his big pale dick jutting out. Then I'm hunched over. Vomit shooting out of my mouth, covering his stomach and dick. Fuck. And I leg it.

He shrieks, 'You're a fucking dead cunt.'

The Virgin Mary makes me think about what it means to want.

The rain comes harder now. I cross town onto John Kennedy Road, over train tracks, iron bars made redundant years before. On the other side the Pilot cinema is boarded up. Makes me think about Mum. Birdee and me sat either side, watching the big screen, our tongues numb from strawberry ice cream.

With dock lights behind, I near the river. Black rain makes it hard to find the line between water and bank. There's a voice beneath the tide that moves dangerously close. My bollocks are throbbing. I hum the nursery rhyme she taught me. But the water gets louder—

The river speaks to me. It sounds like a box of wasps. Swooshing, stirring, spinning lies until I can't stand it. And I know it's not telling me the truth. The river is a lying cunt.

It says to me, How'd you know I'm lying?

Because I do, I say.

Water laughing makes the same noise as shaking a tin of nails.

Tim's trouble, it says.

There, I say, I haven't ever called Fysh "Tim". You're a liar—

Liquid murmurs, I tell the truth.

Go on then.

Hushed at first. Then the wet is gathering, sliding closer, readying itself.

You believe Fysh wants you. And you want him too, it says. But he doesn't. And you're forgetting what the whale told you.

What do you know about that?

The wet whispers, Everything—I know all about the whale.

Water is rushing into my ears. I shout, That's none of your fucking business. But it sounds more like a whisper.

It is my business. Who will you come crying to when he's gone?

Where's Fysh going? I ask.

Under, the water says.

It's all coming into view. I know what the river's getting at. It's not true, I say.

Wrong, it says swirling around, everywhere at once.

And I see that the water flows wherever it wants. Banks don't mean shit.

I say, Get the fuck out of my ears.

The water roars, taunting me. It sings, Row, row, row your boat—

Ditching my muddy trainers at the back door, laces still tied, I leave the trouble outside, where it can stay. Inside are the night noises I am familiar with. They're the same boyhood sounds, but angrier. Mostly it's the weather busting in from the Outer Roads, chipping away at the house bit by bit. It gets beneath the crumbling mortar, rattles the bricks some. Eventually the whole house will fall apart. But not today.

The refrigerator drones, door swung open, while I drink from the milk carton. Beneath my grubby white socks liquid pools. Rain, sweat and river. Splashed in fridge light, I get naked. Stuff clothes into the washing machine and dry the floor with a tea towel before I go upstairs. A crack of light under Birdee's door slows me on the landing, but nothing is spoken. She's mad at me. Not the yell-at-me-kind that makes my neck red and itchy. It's disappointment. She's fed up because I'm being stupid. Stupid comes easy to me.

This room makes me feel miserable. My back against the

wall, I watch Mum's hard green suitcase jammed between the gap made by the wardrobe and chest of drawers. She bought it from the catalogue. Waited a fortnight for it to arrive. Every day looking down the track that runs the length of the river, waiting. I hate that fucking suitcase. Even though the pull to take it is enormous. Go back where I came from. Run away like a chicken-shit.

Birdee is older than me. Taller by two lines marked on the wall beside the back door. We're here watching Mum through the kitchen window, flung open to let the stink out. Breakfast ruined, she's standing out on the track, smoking her packet of cigarettes. One after another. Smoke metallic in the morning light, harassing her. Behind, the river is carrying fishing trawlers to open water, their masts propping up the heavy sky.

'Told you,' Birdee says.

'What's she doing?' I say.

'Waiting—'

'For what?'

'Don't know.'

Birdee bangs the cupboard closed and I'm rinsing out a rag in the sink, squeezing the last drops of dirt until they whirl away down the drain.

'Leave that—' Mum says, closing the door with her bare foot. Places the big brown parcel she's been waiting for on the kitchen table. Peels away the shiny brown tape. Opens up the cardboard box. She lifts out a brand-new suitcase, blue like water where it pools in the shadows of the river-bank. But Mum says it's called teal, 'A colour all on its own.'

14

I don't know about that. 'Looks more blue than green,' I say.

'It's teal—'

'What's it for?' Birdee says.

'Us—' Mum says, and tells me to put it beneath my bed, 'Careful you push it all the way back.'

'Why?' Birdee asks.

'So your father doesn't see it—'

'Alright,' I say.

Later, I don't know how many days for sure, because time by the river runs differently, Birdee busts into my bedroom, says, 'Come on.'

'What's up?'

Outside, Mum is standing on the riverbank in her underwear, the new suitcase on the ground beside her. Maybe she's packed her dress inside? I don't know. Looks like she's waiting for something. Then without a word, she hurls the case into the river. We come and stand beside her. I take one hand. Birdee holds her other. And we watch the water. Her teal suitcase drifting, meant for all three of us.

'Would you believe it?' she says. The tide doesn't want it either; back the case floats, until it's pushed up against the bank. 'Should of filled it with rocks,' Mum says.

'I'll find some,' Birdee says.

'Me, too.' Tugging the suitcase, river rolling off onto thirsty grass.

Mum shakes her head. 'Doesn't matter—' she says.

Blind blackness becomes an angry orange flare. Before I do anything about it, I press my palms against my eye sockets.

Colours flash on the inside of my eyelids, like traffic lights. Red to green and back again. Shivering and damp, I throw off the blanket, find that I have pissed the bed. Bundling the sheets, I go downstairs, closing the kitchen door tight behind me so I don't wake up Birdee. I stuff the ruined bedding into the washing machine on top of last night's wet clothes. Pull off my underpants and include them with the load. Then, because it makes me feel better, I punch the wall. Again, but harder this time. Fucking whale, haunting me.

At the sink I wipe myself down with hot water and the dishcloth. Standing bare, watching the sheets spin around, I listen to the wind testing the windowpanes. What the fuck is happening?

Birdee doesn't say a word about the washing tangled up on the indoor line, turning the ceiling orange. Like we're living beneath a circus tent. Just goes on by me, out the back door. This is her way. She collects pieces of wrongdoing until there's enough to take hold of and make something proper.

When I start the car, she says, 'You look terrible.'

She's not wrong. My eyes are red, itchy with grit. 'Tired is all.' I'm in no mood for this.

'You're in for it—you know?'

'Huh?'

'Disappearing like you did,' she says.

I didn't just vanish. I told my old man I was leaving. 'He knew I was going.' The Mini shakes along the track. It makes my skull ache something terrible. I open the window. Suck in greedy lungs full of river air. Gulls are squawking and carrying on. Can hear the docks waking up. Cranes creaking. Lorries loading.

'It's been two years,' Birdee says.

'I called.'

'Twice—You called twice.'

'And?'

'Close the window,' Birdee says. 'You'll freeze my tits off.'

'Alright—but you know what?' I say, winding out the racket. 'Fysh isn't what you think.'

'Doesn't matter what I think. Besides—who said anything about Fysh?'

'Forget about it.'

We drive the rest of the way without a word. The fan heater blowing a dull tune because the radio hasn't worked since the old man punched it. I go across town, taking Gaywood Road past Saint Faith's. All the while I'm dreading seeing him. Knowing I'm bringing him home to the Point. My stomach rumbles. It's not because I'm hungry. I say to Birdee, 'Thanks—for the peach jelly.'

My old man's not ever been pleased with me. Even when I disappear. He's hated all of my guts for as long as I can remember.

Fucking hospitals. The blue curtains with sharp edges don't hide anything. Not death noises, nor the smell of blood and shit. Doesn't take long to find my old man on the ward. He's dressed, bag packed, ready. The back of his head makes the shape it's always been – stubborn. Birdee reckons my head is exactly the same. I'm inclined to believe her.

There's little room left over in the front pockets of my jeans, but I stuff my hands inside the best I can. Go over to his bed, making the walk harder than it has to be, all the while breathing through my mouth.

'Alright,' I say.

'You're here then—' he says.

Uninterested, he's staring back out the window. Across the aluminium rooftop there's a strip of green that taunts me. If only I could lie down in the grass, start counting blades.

'Nurse said you'd be here an hour ago.'

'Is that right?'

'You home to stay?'

'I am—for now.'

'Right.'

Behind us the ward is busting with sirens. There's barking and feet struggling for purchase on polished floors. Hospitals are fucked up.

'Be a while now,' he says, 'Before they take it out.'

I hate the tiny plastic tube stuck in his arm, held with grubby white tape and dotted with blood. It reminds me of the bleached reeds on the marsh at home giving in to the wind.

'Chairs are over there.'

'Alright—'

T he air, heavy with moisture, turns his red hair to auburn in the half-light. Fysh is wearing baggy black dungarees, messed up with mud and shellfish. I get off Birdee's pushbike, reluctant to let go of the handlebars. Could turn around and ride back out to the house. Leave Fysh alone with his brother, Doug.

'You're late, mate.'

'Yeah—sorry,' I say.

'You all right, or what?'

'I'm good,' I lie. I can't shake the bad feeling I have. What am I doing on the *Ann Marie*? On this stretch of water? 'You got a spare cigarette?'

Fysh fumbles around in the front pocket of his dungarees, tosses me a crushed packet, followed by his lighter. 'Bash on,' he says. 'There's gear for you over there.' He takes a long look at my wet trainers. Shakes his head. 'They won't do, mate.' Takes his lighter back off me.

The boat smells of hot diesel and sweat. I've not been on the *Ann Marie* since Fysh's old man died. There's something about the trawler that unsettles me. The way the fishermen talk without opening their mouths. Fysh says it's because what happens on board, stays on board. Like their stupid superstitions. One time Fysh scolded me for trying to bust open the buttons on his shorts. Told me two men bumming on board's no different from having a woman wreck the trip. I don't know about that. I put on the dungarees, boots and coat he's set aside for me.

Doug asks, 'How's things?' That same uneasy stare.

I blow blue smoke into the air over his head. 'Not bad. You?'

He nods. 'Been better,' he says, glancing at Fysh. 'That right, fella?'

'Nah,' Fysh says. 'We're good.'

Doug is nothing like Fysh. Since we were boys, Doug has circled around me like I'm infectious. Or stink of dog shit. Fysh says it's all in my head. I don't know why brothers pretend things are different from how they really are. It's not like that with Birdee.

The fishing trawler moves to purpose. I hang back, leaning against the winch, watching the backs of the brothers' heads. The engine settles on a dull grind, cutting an easy path through the muddy river, before heading into open water towards Blackguard Sand on the Outer Roads. Here, sea and sky are the same filthy grey, tidewater whirling. The sound of seabirds, great wingbeats, thunder overhead. Seals surface, then dip beneath the wet.

This is the way of shell fishing. The journey out, manoeuvring through a secret place I'm blind to, until we arrive at a patch of water that looks no different from the water on the horizon. But the air here crackles like static on the television. Agitating me.

We're anchored above what Fysh promises is a shedload of catch. I consider how deep it runs. Room enough for a gigantic whale?

'You'll see,' Fysh says. Proud, like a pirate. When he gets excited his cheeks flush. They're the same shade of red they get when he fucks me, just before he cums on my belly.

I sit on a heap of blue coiled rope, knees tucked under my chin. Doug and Fysh have a sawn-down half-barrel a piece, with a plastic up-turned crate for a table. Fysh drinks a can of beer. Doug, tea from a worn yellow plastic flask. I don't want either. We all eat cheese and ketchup sandwiches Doug's missus made the night before. Bread stale and sauce congealed. Fit for the birds circling overhead. I chew, listen to them talk hurriedly about quotas, then in more hushed voices about where the shellfish and shrimp are good. Like I care.

Doug says, 'Heard your old man died.' And now my bollocks start to properly ache.

'Jesus—' Fysh says.

'Not yet,' I say.

I think Doug looks amused, but it's hard to see the line of his mouth beneath his beard. He gets up, goes to the wheel and guns the engine. He manoeuvres the boat in a big circle. Makes one hell of a racket, sending sea-gulls skywards. The prop churns up the muddy seabed. Engine cuts out and the silence is bigger than the space around us.

'Won't be long,' Doug says. Tosses a rake over. I barely

catch it in time. We're waiting for the *Ann Marie* to ground on the mudbank with the ebbing tide in the estuary.

Sat beside Birdee at the lido, I'm waiting for Fysh to turn up. She's found a piece of concrete livid with sunshine to put our towels against. 'Boiling,' I say, using my t-shirt to collect the sweat hounding my forehead.

'Go in the water then,' she says.

'Nah.' I'm agitated. Haven't seen Fysh since we broke up from school three days before. What'll happen now we don't ever have to go back?

From here the pool looks wild. Doug and his trawler mates are messing about. Taking turns trying to drown each other. Even though they're twats, I like looking at them, slinging shiny globs of water all over the place. Once in a while I catch Fysh's brother eyeing us up. 'I reckon Doug fancies you.'

Birdee doesn't even open her eyes. 'He's a cunt,' she says.

'I'm going in—'

'You should.'

The river water washes the heat away. I have my elbows hooked against the edge of the pool, hanging there. Doug backs away from his mate, comes close enough to hear me.

'Alright?' I say.

He looks over his shoulder.

'Fysh coming?'

'No, mate,' he says. 'He's working.'

'Working?'

'That's what I said—you'll have to find someone else to play with,' then he disappears beneath the surface.

I hope he fucking drowns, and I climb out of the water. Lie back down on my towel.

'And—' Birdee says.

'It's nothing.'

'Doesn't look like nothing.'

'You're right,' I say. 'Doug's a cunt.'

She tips on her keel, the motion sending us to our feet. Fysh and Doug take turns throwing equipment overboard onto the mudbank. Heavy knitted blue-nylon sacks, rakes, wooden boards with rope handles either end, and finally themselves down the ladder. I follow them on to the seabed. Fysh's borrowed boots are a size too big for me, heavy in the sodden mud.

Wasting no time, I work quickly to keep warm. Where there's no water, there's nothing beneath to taunt me. Holding on hard, I rock the wooden plank to soften the silt, and pull the cockles to the surface. The brothers work back to back. I'm off to their left, each of us filling our sacks. From time to time I stand up, stretch my sore back, see-saw my shoulders and look about. The unease has worked its way up from my balls to the back of my throat. I can taste vomit there, and old tomato ketchup.

Not the cold. Not our aching muscles. Only the return-ing dirty-brown salt water sliding back moves us off the seabed. Feels like the world has been tipped sideways. Fysh is already hauling the sacks onto the *Ann Marie*, using the chain and winch. Doug is breathing down my neck, making certain all the gear is thrown up. The last sack hits the deck of the trawler; Fysh calls out, 'Come on.'

The tide is galloping on the wind. Now the water is everywhere, threatening and mean-edged. Doug grunts, takes hold of my arm. His grip keeps me tight there. The dark bruises that are his eyes dart left and right as he considers me. 'Fysh,' he says, 'was doing just fine before.'

Somehow I doubt that.

'He tell you about Dora?'

My breath held, the tide washes around the tops of our boots. What about Dora? We need to get back on the fucking trawler.

'She's pregnant.' Shakes his head. 'He needs to be a husband—father.'

If Doug has a point, I wish to hell he'd make it before we both drown. Or worse.

'He ain't thinking about his wife and baby while he's fucking you.'

'Huh?'

'You're a poofter. A fucking little queer.'

I want to headbutt him in the teeth. Though I can't move. I can hear it—laughing at me. It's not far now—

'My brother ain't like you.'

Wrong. He's just like me.

'You had better disappear. Go back wherever you came from,' Doug says. 'And fucking stay there.'

I see everything all at once. The reason why we're standing with the sea rushing around us. Because big-bollocks Doug made it happen. Swallowing the vomit at the back of my throat, 'I'll leave,' I say. Not because I'm afraid of Doug. But what's beneath. It's coming—

'You do that.' And he lets go of my arm. 'I never liked

you. Your whole fucking family are rotten. That crazy bitch sister of yours.'

I want to fucking drown him for bad-talking Birdee. But any moment now—

We wade the distance to the *Ann Marie*. I struggle just behind him, watching the line where his hair meets skin on the back of his neck. He climbs up the ladder on to the *Ann Marie*. Then he reaches down and grabs hold of my hand, pulling me up the ladder and onto the deck. There's relief on board. It can't reach me here.

Fysh, shaking his head, says, 'Bout fucking time.'

Doug slaps him on the back. 'Let's go.'

The *Ann Marie* is roped to the dock when Fysh takes me aside, out of earshot from Doug, says, 'You all right, mate? You've not said two words all afternoon. Doug knackered you out?'

'Something like that,' I say.

He leans in. I can feel the heat of his breath on my cold cheek. 'Wanna come back to mine? I've got beer, and we can go to the chippy.'

I fucking hate chips. I've not told Fysh about Fit Lad and the chip shop. Because it doesn't matter. 'Nah,' I say. 'My old man's back home from the hospital, remember?'

'Shit, yeah.' And he knocks on his forehead with his fist. Looks back over his shoulder. 'I'm as horny as fuck, watching you all day.'

I grin even though I don't feel like it. 'Yeah?'

'Come over.'

'I can't.'

'All right then.' Fysh gives up.

Doug shouts over, 'Catch won't unload its fucking self.'

Fuck you. 'I'm gonna shoot off.' I take Birdee's push-bike from behind a stack of orange plastic crates nestled up against the brick shelter. I ride off. When I look back, Fysh has already moved to unload the catch, but Doug has stopped working to watch me leave.

No money in my pocket for a shedload of work hacks me off. Fuck Doug. I'd be able to stand it but for the river noise pouring into my ear. I'm riding fast, one hand steadying Birdee's pushbike on the stony track, the other, palm pushing against the sound, hammering my head. But it's useless.

The river speaks to me. It slurs, Told you so.

Shut up, I say. Shut the fuck up.

Water growling like a crazy dog, snap-snap-snapping.

Leave me alone.

Cunt, it says, rushing into my ears.

I shake it off, What?

Fysh is a cunt. He went and got her pregnant. Do—ra—Didn't tell you one single word about it.

That's because it's bollocks, I say.

Prove it. Go—on—

I fucking can't, alright? But if I could—

She's all banged up. You think he'll want you afterwards? You suppose he'll have the need to climb on top of you? Whisper fuck-talk into your open ear. Slide his hard—

That's not one bit of your fucking business, I snap.

Is so my business. Who you gonna come crying to when he goes back to her?

He wouldn't do that. And fuck Doug. Doesn't matter

what he threatens me with. Won't make no difference. I'm not giving Fysh up. No way.

Is that so? the river asks. We'll see about that.

You don't know shit.

Quiet at first. Then louder. Row, row, row your boat—

Being here is dangerous. There should be a signpost saying so. The room has no bed. Or a wardrobe to put things inside. Not even a wooden chair remains. Cold walls clawed back to raw plaster. Floorboards spoilt beneath my bare feet, rough and splintered. The windowpanes appear blurred, as if the outside is hurrying by. I might throw up.

My wet red underpants are the only colour here. Beneath the ammonia and mildew is a trace of her smell. Faint and far away. If I close my eyes it crawls closer. My memory of her opens up like weather on the marsh, wild and all at once. Fuck. And I leave her room.

In the bathroom I clean myself up because I have pissed the bed again. But I tell myself it doesn't mean anything. Because it doesn't. Then I rinse out the red underpants and put them on the radiator to dry off. They hang there like a warning. I consider what to do about Doug. I roll the word 'poofter' around my mouth, spit into the basin. Yesterday's threat on the Outer Roads was real. Doug won't rest until he's disappeared me.

There is no way around it. Downstairs, my old man is sitting at the kitchen table. Behind him the window frame's a colourless sky, not unlike the shade of his skin.

'Made you a tea,' he says. 'Heard you walking about.'

I drag out a chair from underneath, and put myself opposite. I am exposed. The tea tastes mean.

'Be cold by now.'

'It's alright,' I tell him.

Between us on the table, a stack of tablets. Small pops punctuate the air, pills lubricated with liquid. The situation is serious.

'You serious about fishing?' his voice low. 'Never imagined you on the water.'

You couldn't imagine me at all. 'Yes,' I lie. 'If they'll have me.' There's no point telling him the truth about the *Ann Marie* now. And that's no bad thing, because I baffle him.

My old man looks into the dregs at the bottom of his mug, searching for something that isn't there. 'You'll be staying, then?'

I nod. A movement so small he'd have to lean closer to catch it. 'Should get going.'

'You fill up the car?'

'I haven't,' I say.

'You'll need to,' he says.

'I'll use the pushbike down to the trawlers. But I'll do it.'

'See you do.'

Outside I duck, expecting the big slab of sky to graze the top of my head. On my right the river cuts a mean line in the brown landscape. I pedal slowly, keeping balance, cold hands stuffed inside my coat pockets. Why the fuck do I believe I'll find any truth here? Seems to me truth hides like rain on the river.

Dockers everywhere at this time, caring nothing about me riding by. I weave in and out, like a loose bottle top getting away. My head's jammed full of rubbish, oil-thick, with no clear view through it, going where my pedals take me.

In town I hide Birdee's pushbike behind a row of blue metal bins and go inside the Bus Cafe. I find a table for two beside a greasy window looking out over the station. There's three lads banging heads, and a woman wearing a purple headscarf. On the table in front of her is a row of scratch cards waiting to be scratched. She looks up and down, past the fluorescent light, hoping God's listening today. Doesn't seem like he hears her, even though the radio is turned down. I recognise the man behind the counter. The tall lad's short mate from the White Hart. His skin in daylight is the colour of spilt milk.

The waitress comes over, takes a chewed-up biro from her apron pocket and writes down my order. 'You want anything to drink?'

'Nah.'

'Suit yourself.'

She smells of fried eggs and chip fat. She hates me because I don't care about her tits. Don't be stupid here, I remind myself. When she walks away I watch her arse. In this place a girl's arse is something you're meant to gander at.

I pull off my coat, hang it on the back of my chair. Because I feel like the three lads are eyeballing me, I switch to the seat opposite. After a while she comes back balancing my fry-up and a plate of toast on one arm. Her other hand drops my knife and fork on to the table.

'Sorry,' she says.

Like fuck. 'Lillian around?'

'Who?'

'Never mind.' And this time I can't be bothered to pretend when she walks away.

I'm three forkfuls into my breakfast. There's banging on the windowpane. This lad outside, arms flapping like a lunatic, is the same as watching a cartoon on television. I call him Hold-Your-Horses, and he likes to suck my dick.

'Heard you were back,' he says, sitting down across from me.

His blond buzz cut looks green in the fluorescent light. My dick gets a little bit hard in my underpants, thinking about his fuzzy head grazing my balls, while he's busy with my hole. 'Here I am,' I say, putting my knife and fork down because I've lost my appetite. 'You been alright?' I don't much care. Last time I saw him I was fucked up and running from Fysh. It was pretty terrible.

'Not bad,' he says. 'Bloody cold out there.'

His breath stinks of cigarettes. There's a dot-to-dot of lively zits on his chin. But he's still nice to look at. Doesn't matter that he's dim like mucky water, and reckons he learned to write reading road signs. 'Cold as,' I agree.

'You gonna eat that?'

'Nah,' I say. Push the plate across the tabletop.

He tucks straight in. Cheeky twat.

'Cheers, fella.'

I stare out the dirty window, watching pieces of

strangers walk past on the other side, thinking about my old man. Now I'm not interested in being here. 'I have to be someplace.'

'You do?'

'You're on my coat,' I tell him.

Hold-Your-Horses passes over my coat. 'Cheers. You know if Lillian still works here?'

'She left—'bout a year ago.'

'Alright.'

He leans across the table. 'You wanna come back to mine later—have some fun?'

'Can't—'

'How come?'

'Cuz—' I say, 'I don't do that shit any more.'

'Bollocks,' he says. 'Seriously? I'm well up for it.'

'Fuck off, alright.' And I get up and go. At the door I almost turn around, wondering if getting my dick sucked would make me want Fysh a little bit less. I keep going.

Outside I hustle Birdee's pushbike along the hard pavement. I'm mad at all of them. I try to decide if they knew I was ruined before I did. My old man had me weighed up. I've never once been able to keep myself from him.

I am a boy. There's a lake of black glass, so still I'm afraid to go nearby in case I mess up the surface. I sit behind my old man on the bank, knees under my chin, watching. He reels in two pike. Little and large. One right after the other. Like magic. Tells me to stay put because he needs to go get more cigarettes from the car. When he disappears behind the brambles, I put my hand into the keep net, careful to mind the teeth, mean as a hacksaw. It's hard at first, but I manage to grip the pike and pull it out of the water. It struggles like it's having a fit. I push the fish down the sleeve of my coat, fold it up into a tight bundle, and place it beside me on the bank.

That's when I consider what's beneath the surface. Hiding. I jump into blackness. Liquid coal chases me. It's quiet here. Until it's not. He takes me from the lake water, up on to the bank. All the while he says, 'You scared the fuck out of me.' Bangs on my chest making a hollow pop, pop, popping sound.

'I'm alright,' I promise, coughing madly.

'You scared the fuck out of me.'

He pulls me along the track by the shoulder of my soggy jumper. Runs heavy, rough hands over my face, scraping the stuck hair from my forehead. He strips me off. Opens the car boot, takes out his big olive parka and wraps it around me. It smells like engine oil and tar soap.

'Get in the fucking car,' he says.

Through the window I watch him walk back down the track, where he collects our things off the bank.

After a time he's finished loading the boot up and taking his soaked clothes off. He gets into the car, and I think his wet underpants look like we've been swimming at the lido together. His big work boots are stupid without his trousers on.

On the ride home he smokes like a bonfire. Rain rushing down the windscreen. Wipers can't keep up. Glancing my way every few miles, to make sure I'm still sat beside him. Each time saying, 'You scared the fuck out of me.'

The week afterwards, I'm sat on the bed, figuring out what to do about the smell stinking out my bedroom.

'Jesus. Smells like something died in here. What've you done?' my old man wants to know.

'Nothing,' I say.

'Bullshit—nothing,' and he's on his knees hunting beneath the bed. He pulls out the wooden first-aid box I found with Birdee. It has a red cross painted on the top. Please don't open it. Inside he sees the dead pike, eaten up with greedy maggots. And the rest.

'Jesus Christ,' he says.

Doesn't matter that I turn twelve tomorrow morning, still he beats me with his belt.

I wanted that pike badly. The way it shone hypnotised me. Some things I've no business collecting. I will tell Fysh that I have to give him up.

T he playground is abandoned. Only two swings rocking across from a broken metal slide. A carrier bag is doing the rounds, whirling this way and that, wind stealing it away down Friar's Street. On the corner, J and I Motor Engineers is boarded up. Grey metal sheets where the windowpanes used to be. The *To Let* sign is spray-painted orange, says *Toilet*.

There's a bum walking in the road, a huge dirty black dog lagging behind him. Closer, I can tell he's wearing a filthy parka two sizes too big, and the dog is really a broken crate, stuffed with black plastic bags he's pulling along on a frayed rope. I consider jumping over the red-brick wall behind me, making my getaway.

He sits down next to me on the bench, says, 'How's it going?'

'Alright,' I say. He's younger than I am. Smells like wet plaster. The metal ring in his eyebrow is infected with crud and yellow shit that makes me gag a little bit. Beneath the mess are fucked-up eyes with lazy lids.

'You're Fysh's mate?'

'Might be,' I say. Who the fuck is this twat?

'I'm Dora's brother,' he says.

'Alright,' I say. Didn't know she had one. 'How's Dora?' Just saying her name makes me feel messed up. I wonder if she knows I'm back in town?

'Dunno.'

I reckon I can smell glue on him.

'That yours?'

'Yeah,' I say. 'That's my pushbike.' Birdee's, to be true.

'Can I borrow it?'

'Nah, mate. You can't.' He's high. Up there with the moon.

'Lend us some money.'

I give Dora's brother the change from my pocket, then ride away.

Church Lane is empty. All Saints' cemetery is mad with weeds and tall grass. The headstones resting lazily against each other, like downed dominos. One has the same orange graffiti taunting the dead. It reads, *Eat me*.

Fysh's cheeks are flushed, nearly as red as his hair. I don't want to tell him that I've been hanging around the Square all afternoon. Pedalling circles. I've seen the sky change colour. Clouds lining up in tidy rows and the stragglers falling behind.

'Where the fuck have you been? What about the fishing today?'

I can't answer the truth of that. Instead I say, 'I'm not fishing for nothing.' And I mean it, because money's tight.

'Doug'd have paid you. But you fucked off before we unloaded,' Fysh says. 'How long you been here?'

'Dunno. Not long,' I say. 'What's it matter?'

He looks at me crooked.

'You never told me Dora has a brother.'

'Who cares?' He has a cigarette in one hand and a canvas bag of fishing gear in the other, tipping him sideways. Smells like sweat and tide mud. Eyes uneasy. 'What the fuck'd you say to Doug yesterday?'

'How'd you mean?' I ask.

'Something he said.'

'Yeah. What'd he say?'

'Said you're leaving. That right?'

'Maybe,' I say. Fuck Doug. Scumbag.

'But—you just got here.'

Get on with this, before you chicken out.

'You coming up, or what?'

'Nah.'

'So what you doing here? Stop messing around.'

'Is Dora pregnant?' I say.

Fysh takes two quick hits from his Benson & Hedges, exhales, says, 'I'm fucked. You gonna stand there like a twat?' He flicks the dog-end on the ground. 'Come on—I'll pay you for yesterday.'

'Doug's right—I'm leaving.'

'You serious?'

'Dora?' The name hangs in the space between, like a scarecrow guarding a winter field.

Fysh hunts around in his head, and comes clean. 'Yeah. She's fucking pregnant, all right. Bollocks. Her brother tell you?'

'Nah. Doug, yesterday on the *Ann Marie*.' Then I walk away with my pushbike because I can't look at his face. But I don't get too far, before he's on me like a shadow.

'Hey—don't just fuck off like that,' his hand heavy on my shoulder, kneading me.

'Get the fuck off.' Because I have to let him go.

'Hold on,' he says. 'Bollocks—just come up already—'

'Fuck you—Fysh,' I shout. Not giving a crap who hears me. Riding hard towards the river, my head is all over the place. Black thoughts leaking out into clenched fists, challenging the miserable flat sky that's doing its best to push me into the tarmac until I'm nothing at all. Why'd he not come after me? I've never not been chasing after him.

I get off my pushbike on the corner of Loke Road, vomit in the alley of number four. I put my forehead against the cold scratchy brick. Stupid. There's no other way with Fysh.

First time Fysh fucks me in the trawler wreck on the marsh, he has me stand this way, manoeuvring me into a place where I'm left guessing what's behind me. Always left wondering what's coming next. My trousers and underpants are around my trainers, and he's rubbing spit into the crack of my arsehole. Hammer hard, holding my breath when he pushes his dick all the way inside me. Hurts something terrible, busts the breath right out of me, but I stand it. Because I like the heat from the palm of his hand pressing against my belly. And just as fast as it starts, the pounding stops. Afterwards, Fysh slips out of the wreck like a shadow being chased by the sun, without saying a word. My arse is wet with cum, and throbs like a bastard. I stay like that in the wreck until I'm sure I won't see the back of him leaving me behind. Before the sun is done with the marsh for the day, I return, and using my penknife I put our initials in the wood. Side by side. So I remember the time I wasn't myself any more.

Two days pass before Fysh is at our back door.

Birdee says, 'Trouble's here.' Puts her back to him.

Fysh's face is purple, and swollen. 'Jesus,' I say. 'What the hell happened to you?'

'It's nothing,' he says.

'Doesn't look like nothing to me.'

'Come on. I wanna show you something.'

'Hang on,' I tell Fysh.

Inside, Birdee's sat back down at the kitchen table, cigarette more ash than paper. 'Changed your mind?' she says.

'Nah, was wondering—' She's doing that thing, keeping quiet, collecting my mistakes for later. Fysh, she believes, is my biggest. I reckon Birdee has figured out he fucked me in the wreck on the marsh. That might be because I look unlike I did before, older than fifteen. Either way, I need her help. 'You still have that cream?'

'I do—'

She knows why I want it. 'Fysh's face—' I'm forced to say. He looks fucked up, and I have to do something about it.

'Doubt it'll help much,' she says, tucking her hair behind her ear. 'In my room.'

After I've collected her cream, halfway outside, Birdee yells, 'Coat—'

I lean around the back door and do as I am told.

'What's all that about?' Fysh asks.

'Nothing,' I say.

He hops up on my handlebars because he walked here from town. We ride like that along the track, river on our right, a muddy line against the rotten riverbank. His coat smells of cigarettes and damp. Beneath this a trace of skin and armpits.

When we get to Black Barn, Fysh gets off. Says, 'Come on.' He holds back the black corrugated iron, careful not to slice his fingers, while I slip through the gap. I use my trainer to kick it aside for him. The light in here struggles for purchase.

'You reckon that retard really buried a man here?'

'I fucking guarantee it,' he says, climbing the ladder.

That's when a piece of metal, ripped from the roof, lets past a slice of light that strikes his hair. Looks like a burning match.

'You coming up? Or what—?'

'Alright,' I say, a little bit bewildered.

Up top Fysh is lying on a dirty heap of blankets, beneath the split in the roof, smoking. His arm is holding the back of his head, reminding me of the sunbathers at the lido.

'What happened?' He looks at me like I'm talking in tongues. 'Your fucking face?'

'Some wanker nicked my bike,' he says. 'Did this—'

'Fuck,' I say. Even though I don't believe him. 'Does it hurt?'

'Know what'd make it better?'

'Fuck off.'

'What'd you reckon?'

'About what?'

'This—' Meaning the blankets he's brought here. For us.

'Dog's bollocks,' I tell him. Because it is. 'Got you this—'

'What is it?'

'For your bruises.'

'Don't matter,' he says. 'Doesn't hurt.'

I unscrew the cap and squeeze a glob onto my finger. Then I lean in. Fysh leans back. 'Don't be a twat.' I rub cream carefully into each bit of bruised skin, until he looks sweaty, likes he's been running. 'That ought to do it,' I say. 'What's wrong—does it sting?'

'Nah,' he says. 'But now look—'

Fysh has no interest in hiding his hard-on. His gaze taunts me. Even messed up and shiny he's something else.

I get busy cheering him up. While outside, the wind whines.

Using my coat sleeve, I wipe vomit from my chin, hoping whoever lives behind window number four doesn't come out and beat the crap out of me for messing up their alley-way. Get back on my pushbike. Slick with rain, Cross Bank Road arrows through the middle of Alexandra Dock. There's angry red shipping containers stacked along the route to keep trouble out. Tankers, twin grain silos and shed twenty-five ruin the view beyond. Past dock sounds, the quay mudflats are littered with fishing trawlers, their booms tangled up with iron, rigging and purpose. Gulls grounded, the air is stale with rotten shellfish and tide mud. Covered in graffiti, the brick shelter keeps the wet

43

off fishermen who have returned from fishing the Outer Roads, sharing cigarettes and measured words. Here, the ache spreads out beneath my skull. But at the river proper, the water wails—

T he river speaks to me. Dora— Dora— it yips.

What about her? I say. What do you know about it?

Do—ra— it says.

Fuck you. Stop messing around.

She hates Fysh. You should hate him, too.

You know nothing about it.

When he's inside you, breath burning your neck, he sees her face on the back of your head.

That's bollocks. Bollocks—

It's true— Fysh's a bad man. Water giggles. You get hard for him. You shouldn't.

Go away—

Don't be childish. You think hands clamped over your ears can keep me out?

Maybe, I say. Or maybe I'll pour petrol onto you, and fucking set you on fire.

River says, Who are you fooling?

Leave me alone. Get the fuck out of my ears. Stop speaking to me.

Gurgling noises. A faint whisper. Row— Water swishing. Running. Pouring—

Alright, I say, I give up.

The water says, So easily?

Fuck off. I'm serious, I say.

So am I, its dirty tongue lapping.

What do I do? Tell me.

How am I supposed to know? the river runs.

I thought you would.

What do you want me to tell you?

The truth—

How about you tell me what you're running from?

A great big fucking whale, I say. You already know that—

The water whispers, But it's dead. It can't hurt you.

Wrong— I shout. Wrong— The dead are the only ones that can—

What's Birdee say about that? the river asks, roaring—

Fysh is on the other end of the telephone, telling me I'm a big twat for clearing off today without giving him a chance to explain himself. He's hacked off, and being a loudmouth. Sounds like he's been drinking some cans, because when I cross the kitchen to the fridge, letting the phone hang on its grubby cord, I can still hear him bashing on while I slug cold milk from the carton.

'You even listening to me?' he wants to know. 'Cos you ain't saying much.'

'I am.' He reckons I should drive over, right now. I can't be bothered to tell him the Mini won't start because I forget to get petrol again. 'My old man's gone back into hospital,' I say. There's a note on the table written in blue biro.

The line crackles and pops like it does on television when the law are listening in. 'I'll drive over—now,' he says. 'Stay put.'

I don't know if this is what I want. 'Alright—' I hang up the telephone. So much for giving him up. We're something unnatural, glued shoulder to shoulder, like a freak that people'll pay money to gawp at.

I put the milk back in the fridge. What about my old man? If he'd died somebody would have told me. I take the piece of paper, screw it up into a tight ball. And bin it.

When I open the back door to Fysh, first thing out of his mouth, 'Sorry—about your old man.'

Somehow sounds like he's been practising what to say on the drive over. Fysh does this when his head is whirling with worries and he can't settle on one trouble at a time. A big mess.

'You drunk?' I ask.

'Course not, mate,' he says.

By the look of him he's sat and stewed since I fucked off earlier. Wild eyes, and there's an angry fist-shaped blotch on his forehead. He sits down at the kitchen table, and pulls the tab on a can of beer. 'Can I use your bath? I stink like the fucking *Ann Marie*,' he says.

Fizzing noises, and I'm licking my lips. Fysh slides the pack across the table towards me. But I leave it there. My back against the sink, arms folded across my chest. 'Bath takes ages to fill,' I say, and leave him drinking.

After a while Fysh comes upstairs, into the bathroom, pulls his sweatshirt off, and chucks it in a heap on the floor. 'Certain things grate on my fucking mind,' he says, rubbing the centre of his bare chest. He kicks his trainers off without untying the laces. His white socks could be yesterday's. 'It's bollocks. The whole thing.' He runs his hands through unruly red hair. 'Fuck.' Changes tack like he's navigating shallow water on the Outer Roads, tugging the waistband of his trackie bottoms until I can see two inches of black underpants and red pubic hair. 'It's nothing, mate.'

With Fysh, nothing isn't ever nothing. I'm getting close to dangerous. I've been here before with him. Makes the line where my hair meets the skin on my neck itch. I say, 'You smell really bad.'

Fysh gets naked and climbs into the bath water. I sit down on the plastic toilet seat, light a cigarette, hand it to Fysh, and light another for myself. His skin is luminous under the naked bulb. He blows blue smoke rings that rise to the ceiling before disappearing into the damp plaster.

Fysh is complicated. 'Can't ignore this. There's no way round it,' I say. 'This is serious.'

'Yeah, I fucking know that.'

The window above the bath is a perfect pitch-black square, like a chalkboard waiting for class. I have an itch to write *Do You?* into the condensation gathering there. Maybe then he'd see the long stretch of trouble laid out ahead of us.

'Pregnant. Why wouldn't you tell me something like that?'

He pushes his palms against eye sockets, says, 'Fuck. Lads like us don't want much.' Then leaning forward, arms on knees, 'Why'd you stay away so long? Two fucking years.'

'You know why. It's what you wanted.'

His face is surprise chasing after want. A big ache. As if he's trying to see what's out there, past everything he's already seen. 'You were gone. But you didn't get far.'

'Far enough,' I say. But really Fysh is not wrong. Leaving here was like throwing stones at the wind.

Fysh turned twenty-two today, and we're on his bed messing about. We are meant to be at the Greenland getting pissed up with his brother, Doug. But Fysh said he wanted to have some fun now, because later he'd be fucked up. Covers kicked off, he has one arm wrapped around my neck, pinning me here. While working a big glob of spit into my asshole. Then Fysh pushes his dick against me, taking his time, until he's ball-deep. I yelp, but it's muffled by the mattress. He fucks me for ages.

Afterwards, the light in his bedroom fading fast. Fysh eases himself over until he's half off me. His nose nearly nudging mine, 'Guess what?' he says. His expression unfamiliar.

'What?'

'I'm—getting married.'

'Huh?'

'It's true.'

I make to move, but Fysh keeps me here with the urgency in his eyes. Sometimes being with him is like trying to push back the river with my palms. There's too much to hold on to. He pours through me and I'm soaked with him. 'Don't understand,' I say.

'Yeah—you do,' he says. 'Me and Dora haven't been a secret.'

Maybe, but I didn't think it mattered. All of a sudden I reckon I might throw up. 'It's a lot,' I say.

Fysh nods. 'I know.'

'This us over, then?' And I'm bawling a little bit.

'Nah—this is us adjusting,' he says.

'How'd you mean?'

Fysh frowns, 'Dunno. Like fishing, I guess. You go where the catch is.' He tells it like it is. 'It's what they expect me to do.'

Now I'm crying properly. But no sound comes out. 'Alright,' I say. But nothing will be.

'Jesus,' Fysh says, brushing my eyebrow, running his thumb back and forth, following the arch. 'What would you have me do?'

I'd have him get that trawler he talked about. Bust out on his own. Forget what he reckons is the road laid out before him. Now Fysh is crying too. 'Don't.' And we lie like two twats watching one another.

Sometimes I think this is my favourite part of sleeping with Fysh. Just being alongside, listening to his breath lap back and forth like the river. He's on the edge of sleep. I reckon later, in the Greenland, we'll look like two normal lads necking pints. Nobody will know what happened here on this messed-up bed. But beneath the table Fysh will deliberately glue his knee to mine. And if I were a girl, it would be the same as holding hands.

'Water's getting cold,' Fysh says. Picks at the scab softening on his knee. 'I never knew I wanted a kid—until she told me.'

'What's that supposed to mean?' I say.

'I didn't know it mattered.'

Me neither. Like he read my head, he says, 'The *Ann Marie*—this life fishing. It's what I am.'

'I know what you are—'

'Don't do that. Don't be that twat. I don't make the fucking rules.'

'Alright' I say.

'Listen,' Fysh explains. 'I see what you're getting at. But can't I want both?' There's something in his eyes that's worse than trouble. Or grief. I think it might be hope. 'I'll be a father—'

What everyone wants him to be. Maybe he'd be a good father? Better than my old man, for sure. 'What about Dora?'

He slugs the beer can, stands the empty on the edge of the bath beside the soap. 'Me and Dora, we're done in the way you're worrying about.'

'Where's she now?'

'No fucking clue, mate.'

'You worried?'

'Nah, I'll find her.' Fysh knocks at his forehead. 'She's changed. Something's different.'

'What?'

'Dunno,' he says. 'But she'll come around.'

'How'd you mean?'

'There's rules. She knew what she was doing, marrying a fisherman.'

Fucking fishermen and their stupid rules. 'What about Doug— He reckons if I don't fuck off, he'll see to it himself.'

'Doug's all fucking talk.'

'Nah,' I shake my head. 'He means it.'

'I can handle Doug.'

'You think you can handle Doug?' I've never seen Fysh

handle his brother. Not one time. 'What the fuck are you doing?'

'What's it look like, mate?'

'You really wanna be doing that—right now?'

'What'd you reckon? Beats the crap out of this bollocks,' he says. Through the bathwater there's his hard-on, the head of his dick almost breaking the surface, daring me down there. 'Stop talking. Get the fuck in here. Let me worry about Doug.'

Useless arguing. Fysh does this to me. Right now all I can see is what's right in front of me. As though he's hypnotised me. Taken me someplace where there's no choice but to peer over the edge to see what's hiding there. Even if it means falling off.

'You're an idiot,' I say, pulling off my t-shirt and trousers. Already hard, I step into the bath with him. When I sit down the spare water sloshes over the side on to the floor.

'You've still got your shreddies on,' he says.

'Yeah,' I say. 'I know.'

'Twat.'

Fysh only ever kisses me when he's drunk. And I'm still grinning when he leans forward, one hand holding the back of my head, his tongue hot in my mouth. He's gentle, like I'm brand new. I wish I'd brushed my teeth. His mouth tastes like trouble. My tongue hunting around after every last drop. I pull away, ask, 'You alright?'

'Yeah,' he says, 'Little bit wasted.'

T he river yips, telling tales that drive me from the house. Sky is nothing much to see, all colour wrung out.

Bed abandoned, I stand in Fysh's trainers, wiggling my toes because they're a size too big for me. Fysh is somewhere inside the house. It's bone cold in just my underpants, while I shout at the river. 'Where are you?' The brackish tidal water slides around, looking curious. The light has barely climbed up onto the marsh. 'What do you want?' I yell. 'Tell me—'

Nothing. The river's taunting me. Like it did Mum.

I am smaller. Mum has us on the riverbank. We're holding hands like a paper cut-out, barefoot and wild. Her long pale hair, a single patch of brightness between us. She asks, 'Can you hear it?'

Big-eyed, Birdee glances from the black line of river over at me. I can't hear it either. The river makes no sound, bank damp and still.

Mum sighs. 'Neither of you hear it?'

Because she feels bad, Birdee says, 'I hear it—now.'

'Me—too,' I say.

Mum looks from me to Birdee, shakes her head. We stand like that until the light comes proper, watching her listen to nothing, humming a gloomy tune.

At the back door, home from his shift at the factory, my old man watches and waits. A dark stain against the white wall. Looking baffled.

'What the hell have you been doing out there?' he says.

'Picking flowers,' Birdee says.

From the top of the refrigerator Mum takes down a cloudy glass jar, the rim chipped, and fills it with Birdee's purple flowers. She runs tap water into the jar. Places it on the windowsill above the sink.

'Al—ice. Al—ice,' he barks. It's how he talked to the dog, before the tide took him away. 'You hear me?' He picks up the jar of flowers, throws it hard at the floor. Big bang, glass and purple everywhere. Shattered and pretty. 'Out on the riverbank like a lunatic.' When she turns around, he blows smoke in her face. 'Crazy. Doesn't make no sense.' Stubs out his dog-end on the draining board. Fizzing in the wet.

Mum stands still, mesmerised by the mess.

'Careful—' I say.

Three strides across the kitchen floor, glass grinding. 'Or what?' He points a finger at me, nail chewed down and nicotine-stained. Drilling into the middle of my forehead.

'The glass—we'll cut our feet.'

'I'll get the brush,' Birdee says.

'You do that,' he says. 'More use than your mother.'

With our old man out the way, Birdee sweeps up his mess. Mum watching the world outside the window, smoking her cigarette.

'Where you going?' Birdee says.

'Pick more flowers,' I say, heading on out to the riverbank to hunt down her purple.

I spit onto the mud. My mouth tastes of last night's beer and cum. Unable to hold it back, I vomit over Fysh's trainers. Chin messed up, I say to the river, Fuck you. For taking her away.

Inside, the house is still. I guzzle cold water in the kitchen. Scoop a palmful to rinse the mess from my face, sleep from my eyes. Then head on upstairs.

I find Fysh naked, sprawled on his back on my old man's bed. The room is still and wrong. I tear back the curtains. Crack open the window to let the wind rush in.

'Jesus Christ, Fysh. Get up.' I try and remember if he fucked me in my old man's bed last night, but the effort hurts. In the morning light his pale skin looks like putty, his red hair never brighter. His mouth and cheek are ruined with dry vomit. Too fucked up to clean himself. 'Fysh,' I say, shaking him. He's cold. I don't know why I didn't see straight off that his eyes are cracked open. Colourless. I want to hold his hand. But I'm afraid to. There's a terrible sensation in my balls. I have nothing inside left to throw up. So I stand very still. I say to him, 'You're dead—Fysh.'

*

I am straddling a dead man. In my hand his balled-up t-shirt, soaked with tap water. Wiping him clean. Bit by bit. Until he's himself again. But his ears are deaf to me. Bawling and pleading. This I know—dead things don't always stay dead. My face is close to his face. There's a line of spit and snot joining his bottom lip to my open mouth. Fysh. His eyes have forgotten what colour they're meant to be. Where'd the fuck it disappear to? How can it not be there any more? Everything goes away.

Now and again the breeze through the window lifts a piece of his red hair off of his forehead then lets go again. It might just be the worst thing I've ever seen—

Because I am braver now, I slide off Fysh and lie alongside him. Our bodies lined up like toy soldiers. He looks awake from here, like he can see past the plaster on the ceiling to the sky outside, and further. I lean across and kiss him on the cheek. Fysh.

'I'm sorry,' I say, because I'm acting like a fucking poofter.

It's time, I say for him.

'Not yet—' I answer myself. I'm not ready for the law. The questions. Any of it.

Alright, mate. We'll just lie here a bit longer. If you like?

'What you thinking about?' I ask.

Getting my own boat, he says. Imagine that?

'You should do it.'

Got the name all planned out—

'Yeah—Yeah—' I tell the dead lad lying beside me.

*

We're on the riverbank first time Fysh owns me. Our push-bikes tangled up together. In the distance I can see Black Barn, hunkered down like a dog taking a shit. Sunlight all over the place, getting in our eyes. Here there's scorched grass grazing bare backs. Fysh has one arm cradling his damp head, chest sticky with sweat. His armpit smells of pencil shavings. And I'm keen enough to stay here for a while. He's staring up at the sky, watching the line an aeroplane has drawn across the blue, telling me about some big plan he has for getting his own fishing trawler. Cutting loose from his family and the *Ann Marie*. Says he's gonna call it *Joe*.

'Yeah, yeah,' I tell him. 'Stop messing about.' Fysh makes promises like trees grow leaves.

'Nah,' he guarantees. 'I'm not messing with you,' turns his face towards me and winks. 'Soon as I'm eighteen.'

But there's a wide-open grin there, hypnotising me. I tell myself it's not just because he's happy with having his dick sucked dry at Black Barn. That there's more to it than cum-promises.

T he river speaks to me. It says, —Death.

    I say, What do you know about death? Tell me—

    More than you, the river says. Much more. It babbles, lapping, murmuring his name. It says, Tim— Tim—

Call him by his name, I shout. His name is fucking Fysh.

Was Fysh, the water says.

Yes, I say, Was—Fysh.

That's right, Was—

You took him away from me, I say. You fucking killed him. Drowned him in his own vomit. Why'd you do that? Why'd you take him? I shout. What was the fucking reason?

The river is angry, tide rushing now. It roars, Some things just are. The whale warned you—

I—was—his—you fucking cunt. His—

Now calm all at once, it says, No. You were never his. He belonged to Dora.

You're lying, I say. The dead whale lies too. All you do is fucking lie to me.

No, it says. He was Dora's. Do—ra—

Mine first, I say. I miss him terribly.

Water giggles, says, You miss him inside you. Fucking you.

Go away.

The heat, it says. You liked the pain, too.

Yes, I say. So what? I miss him fucking me, alright. I don't know what to do.

That's easy. Find someone else to fuck you. Hold-Your-Horses— Fit Lad—

Why'd you say that? To make me feel worse? I hate you. You don't hate me, it says. That's impossible.

I'll never speak to you again. Not ever. You're a cunt.

Quietly rippling, just a wet whisper, but it gets louder, deeper, deafening— Row, row, row your boat, gently down the stream. Merrily, merrily, merrily, merrily, life is but a dream. Over— and over— and over—

'**D**on't say a fucking word,' Doug warns. He turns off the engine, chucking the car into bare silence. We get out. Above us, the massive asbestos roof blocks out the sky, filthy black and furious. He walks ahead of me, following an iron track flush with the ground. Behind me his agitated mate is on my heels, yipping like high tide. I consider running. But where to? I'm edged up beside an expanse of wartime brick on my right, my left an industrial wasteland. Concrete, weeds, and smashed-up work huts where losers sniff glue. He's brought me to the Muck Works, south of town. This place is forgotten on purpose.

'Keep moving,' his mate says, pushing against the small of my back.

'Not long now,' Doug says. Teeth grinding, shoulders see-sawing.

In my head I reach around to figure out how much time has come and gone. How long—between Fysh and here?

*

Everything is further away than it's meant to be, misplaced. Fysh's really red hair. Ghosts dragging me awake. The window cracked open. Bawling in the dent he left behind in my old man's bed. My memories muddled. Like being small on the riverbank playing cat's cradle with Birdee. Her telling me I'm doing it wrong. But she doesn't hold it against me. Tangled, until some clever twist unties my fingers. Coming undone. The whale's warning drifting in from the river.

Still, it's hard to hold the string of hours. I know the law came on the first day. Took me away. Sucking cigarettes until my lips sting. Brought me back. Two days I reckon, Fysh has been dead. Now I'm wearing his clothes because they smell like him—

Doug and his mate are leading me to the pit. A stagnant green bottomless hole in the ground, filled with rainwater, and old fertiliser from the works. Fysh beat up Vinnie Foreman here, after he called us two bent poofters in school. Hasn't changed much.

All the while playing on my mind is how did Doug take me. 'You break into my house?' I say.

'Nah, you dumb fuck,' his mate says. 'Door was wide open.'

Fuck. Ahead of me the hole appears lifeless and stonestill. Burying the truth beneath the surface. More like a big oil stain on the concrete slab than a body of water. What does bottomless really mean? Looks like I'm about to find out.

'Stop,' Doug says.

There's a burnt-out Volkswagen Beetle driven up to the edge. Gaps where the headlights used to be look like eye sockets, an angry dog guarding a patch of ground.

'Undress.'

Beside his boots is a can of petrol from the *Ann Marie*. 'Get fucked,' I say.

Doug's mate punches me in the back of my head. It's not hard, but topples me forward, shortening the space between me and the pit.

'Not gonna ask twice,' he says.

His mate says, 'You fucking heard him, bender.'

I kick off my trainers. I'm not wearing any socks. Then Fysh's sweatshirt. Trackie bottoms next. I thought I'd feel colder, but I don't somehow.

'And the rest.'

I take off my underpants, covering myself with my hands. The familiar ache in my balls.

'What—now?' I ask.

Doug flips. 'Guilty—as fucking charged. You're not even denying it. You killed my little brother.'

'No,' I say.

'Liar.'

'Nah—I'd never hurt Fysh—I—'

'I don't wanna hear that queer fucked-up shit,' he yells, our noses grazing.

I will die today. Right fucking here. My eyes are hunkered down tight. I'm not afraid. But I won't look at Doug, because it's what he wants.

'Fucking admit it. You killed him—you little poofter.'

Jaw bolted shut. I won't answer him. It's what he needs.

Fuck him. He's spraying my face, spit and hot breath trying to bust open my eyelids.

Screaming, 'Cunt—'

His first punch puts me square on the ground. Kicks me in the mouth, gut, tries for my bollocks, but I won't loosen my grip. Takes hold of my hair, starts dragging me across the concrete, tearing up my backside. Raging and growling, pulling me closer to the water's edge. 'You're fucking dead.'

'Doug?' His mate interrupts. 'Petrol—'

Everything stops. His mate brings over the can of petrol, placing it on the ground beside his boots. 'Open it,' Doug says, not taking his eyes off me. 'Here—pass it over.'

Where my skin is broken, blood and fuel explode. The pain is terrible, winding me. Worse than the ache in my bollocks. I don't want to die here, alone. Doug stops pouring liquid when the can runs dry. My eyes sting like hell with the stench, streaming. Tongue tasting of petrol, iron and fear.

'Lighter,' Doug says, turning his head, fingers clicking.

Here's my chance. I let loose my balls. Push my hands hard against the cold concrete for purchase, kick out, giving everything I have. Crunch. Doug shoots backwards, banging into his stupid mate. And they're gone. Disappeared like a shadow when the light goes out. As if I'd imagined the whole thing. But I haven't.

Pulling myself up, stumbling in a mad circle, I'm hunting for my trackie bottoms and trainers. They're heaped beside the empty petrol can.

'You're fucking—' Doug roaring like a lion, head and shoulders above the oily mess.

I tug on my trainers, and boot the can, aiming for Doug's red head. It whistles past his ear, thumping into the pit. Doug's gone again. Dragged under by his drowning mate. I hope they both fucking die.

Bollock-naked, bolting across the wasteland like the law are chasing after me. Praying to Jesus Christ—that he knows where the old man has stashed his rifle. Hoping Fysh'll forgive me—his cunt brother leaving me no other way out.

Birdee is thirteen the first time the old man makes her fire the rifle for real. She shivers with unshed feelings because she doesn't want to kill the rabbit. 'You're not a child,' he tells her.

He's wrong. Standing still behind her, I can see the rabbit in the distance, a brown smudge against the silvered marsh. Frost overnight has laid a fine blanket of sharp ice everywhere. I want to kill the rabbit for her. To take away the ache he's leaving inside her that'll grow into stone. Yet I don't. Because I can't.

Boom. And Birdee misses. Big black wings alongside us rush skyward. The old man takes the rifle out of her hand, slaps her hard across the face. 'You'll not miss on purpose again,' he says.

Birdee doesn't cry. Looks on over at me, blank as night. But inside I know she's smiling.

Here I am in the half-light, holding my breath, aiming my old man's rifle at Doug. I've been expecting him. Should've slashed all four tyres.

From here I can see it all. His mate in the passenger seat. Can't hear what they're arguing about. Boot flipped, and Doug rummaging around inside. Coming away with a big shiny hammer in his hand. He wants to smash my head in. Even the river's tipping the bank for a closer look.

I want to kill Doug dead. But what would Fysh have to say about it? I fire a shot. Dirt busting apart, biting his boots and shins. He jumps backwards, slamming into the car door. Surprise on his face sliding into rage. He's covered in shit from the filthy water. 'Bird—ee—'

Stick my head out of the old man's bedroom window. I warn him, 'You fucking breathe near her—you're dead.' Fysh'll have to understand.

'Crazy cunt,' Doug yells, 'We're not finished.' He slips round the car, back behind the wheel, and starts the engine. Then his stupid mate gets out, darts over to Fysh's car like his balls are on fire, climbs inside. Car's been parked on the riverbank since he came over that night.

I stay watching until the dust settles into shadow. Relieved that Birdee is safe with the Soldier.

When the night comes, I move outside. Still stinking of blood and petrol, I start a fire.

The heat from the oil drum rushing across my sore skin. I watch the flames lick apart everything, until there's no trace left. Clothes from the Muck Works. My old man's sheets that Fysh fucked me on. All gone. Sparks chasing after each other until they burn themselves out.

Above, the night is black and calm. Tonight I'll sleep

with my old man's rifle in my own room. It will be dream-less. And in the morning I will go see Dora, now I know where she is. Tell her that Fysh is dead.

D own from Our Lady of the Annunciation, off London Road, is a terrace of neglected three-storey red-brick houses. Number ninety-three has a pale green door, paint peeling, framed by ruined plaster columns blackened with petrol fumes. I push the doorbell. And again, because it looks like it might be broken. What the fuck is she doing here?

I can hear somebody on the other side of the door. This time I bang twice with the edge of my fist. Opening up, the man in front of me is taller than I am, wearing stubble and a worn purple t-shirt. His eyes are hooded. Lips bruised. 'Fuck off, mate.'

'Wait,' I say, inching forward. 'I need to see Dora.'

He doesn't like me. 'Like I said, mate. Fuck off already.'

'Tell her—' What do I say? 'She needs to come talk to me. Or I'll tell Fysh she's here. Tell her that.'

I think he wants to punch me in the head. 'And who the fuck—oh—you're him, right?'

I don't like that this twat knows about Fysh and me. 'Yes.' I'm him.

Now I'm waiting, back pushed up against the column, wondering who called me up on the telephone to tell me where Dora's been hiding out. Told me someone needs to do the right thing about her dead husband before she reads it in the local rag. He's a stranger. No one I've heard from before. But he's right, I guess it should be me. And yet I want to leg it out of here.

'Okay,' he says. 'Come—on.'

Dimly lit, I follow him up a wide staircase, his arse in my face. The pocket of his black jeans has been torn clean off, leaving a square of white underpants looking out. 'Take a load off,' he tells me.

Yellowed, paper-thin curtains cast a greasy haze over the room. An electric fire glows orange in the hearth of a marble fireplace. Sash windows rattle after a lorry hammers by on the road outside. The air in here is thick with bleach and old plaster. I'm not alone.

Across the room a pasty skinhead eyeballs me, his dick worked half-hard in the palm of his hand. He's one arm draped around a scrawny girl, her body shaped like a boy's, with small sharp tits. 'You up for it, fella?'

Her face is smudged, like she's really a cartoon he's already started to rub out. No wonder she wants to disappear. He looks like a proper twat. 'Nah—' I tell him.

'Your loss, fella.'

I put my back to the situation, treading a troubled floor, struggling to figure out a way to tell Dora terrible things.

*

72

'Upset her—I'll break your teeth,' the man in the purple t-shirt warns me.

I don't know who he is to Dora, but he's somebody. 'Alright,' I say.

Showtime. Dora is standing in the doorway, says my name like she's announcing a circus act in the big tent. Then, 'How the fuck'd you find me?' Dora never was much for small talk.

'Dunno.'

'Fuck off if you're here to play games.'

'I'm not,' I say.

She's trying to work out if I'm trouble or not. 'Fysh do that—to your face?'

'Nah,' I shake my head, ignoring her question. 'It's important. I wouldn't be here if it wasn't.'

'Not here,' she says.

We go downstairs, along a dark hallway, through a dirty kitchen, stinking of fish and chips, out into a narrow back-yard. The yard is bitter and damp, fucked up with sodden cardboard boxes and a washing machine missing its door.

Dora takes a packet of crumpled cigarettes out of her pocket, and lights one. 'Fysh really not know I'm here?' The smoke lingers for a bit, hiding her mood.

'Nah.' He doesn't know anything any more.

'Out with it,' she says. 'What's so bloody important? I'm guessing the state of your face has something to do with it?'

'Kind of,' I say. 'Doug did this.'

'Damn every fucking one of them,' she says. 'Why're you here?'

'Fysh.'

73

'I figured that much out.'

I feel like a chicken-shit. A poofter. My mouth hung open, nothing coming out.

'What about him?'

Because I can't find another way, I just have to say it. 'Fysh is dead.' I want so badly to take it back. Run someplace else. But my feet won't move. 'He's gone—'

Dora narrows her eyes, until I can't see any blue there no more. Takes two short drags of her cigarette, says, 'The *Ann Marie*. He drown?'

Shake my head. 'Three days ago,' I tell her. My face hurts, eyes aching something terrible. 'Drowned in his own puke,' I get out. 'At the Point, in my—' Now I'm bawling a little bit. Heavy arms hugging myself. Fucking freezing here.

A crow squawking cracks the silence.

'You in trouble?' she asks.

'Some,' I say. 'Law let me go. But Doug's after me—reckons it's my fault.'

'Fuck him—'

'I'm sorry, Dora. I—'

'You need to go.'

'Alright,' I say. But I have to tell her. 'I've not told anyone you're here. But—they'll be looking for you.'

She opens the latch on a tall blue gate; I pass her by, hear the latch clip behind me. If she's crying, there's no sound, only my trainers on the wet stone, and the miserable crow cackling.

N ight is a different place, in-between everywhere else. This is where I am, drifting in the current. Sometimes Fysh is here with me, red hair a beacon above his taut, pale back. He won't turn around, no matter how much noise I make. Or flap my arms. But I keep watch, in case he slides into the shadows for good.

The noise from the television interrupts us. I am returned, listening to the madness trapped inside a black box. My eyes have nothing to watch except static, anaemic wasps flying at night, because the aerial's come undone from the rooftop. Wind's been blowing in off the Outer Roads something fierce, hammering the house.

I'm on the couch in underpants that need changing. I can smell my armpits. My throat is sore from too many packs of cigarettes. Now I'm up, I need a drink.

In the kitchen I run the tap, scooping up mouthfuls of cold water to ease the burning. The old man's rifle beside me on the draining board. This is what it means to be hunted.

There's no one here to talk to. 'That's a good thing,' I

say. It's strange to hear my voice outside of my head. Birdee is with the Soldier. My old man in the hospital.

I can see myself in the black glass window. I am disgraceful. 'Doesn't matter.'

Behind me the telephone busts its bell. 'Hello?'

All I can hear is water running, gurgling, seeping through the line. I bang it back in its cradle on the wall. Fucking cunt river. 'Stop calling me.'

When this happens I pull on my coat, step into Fysh's trainers, unbolt the back door, and move into deep night. The cold and wind sharpen me. An owl hoots. There's the taste of salt on my tongue. Marsh grass scratches my bare legs. After I've circled the house, tried the shed door, I slip into the Mini, leaning the old man's rifle on the passenger seat. I want to drive down the track, look for any sign of Doug. But the car won't start. 'Fuck.'

The headlights are chucking yellow light along the track, leaking into the bushes one side, the riverbank the other. The water is silent. I am stupid because I forgot to fill up with petrol. There's no trouble here, even if I have itchy bollocks. Doug has not come back for me this night.

'Petrol can,' I tell myself.

The back door is groaning in the wind, hanging open because I've come inside to collect the shed key, when the ringing telephone rattles. 'I said stop fucking calling—'

Man says, 'Funeral's tomorrow.'

It's him. The stranger. He sounds nearby, as if he's really hiding on the other side of the wall in the hallway, trying to trick me. 'You called me before. About Dora.' Why'd he do that?

'Yeah—I called before.'

'Fysh's funeral. Why'd you care?'

'I figured—you'd want to know. That's all.'

'Who are—' He hangs up before I finish.

I reckon it's an hour's walk to the all-night petrol station on South Gates roundabout, could be more. Should probably put on some trackie bottoms, maybe a pair of socks, get going. I have to be there. Fysh's funeral, tomorrow morning.

I want to see his face. The engine's still running; we're parked on Pilot Street. From here I can see Saint Nicholas's Chapel, the spire stretching up into thunderheads, piercing the grey.

The service started a while back. We watch half the town turn out for Fysh's funeral. Disappearing into the church in twos and threes, wearing borrowed hats and dark coats. Fucking hypocrites. Pretending they don't know he drowned in cum and beer. Tide never came near him. These townies are all the same. Sons catching more hate from their fathers than shellfish. Around it goes like the gallopers at the Mart.

'You can't—go inside,' Birdee says. She's wearing her best blue coat, hair tucked neatly behind her ears. 'Doug'll kill you.'

'So fucking what,' I say. I'm mad at her for staying away until this morning. 'Surprised you're here. And not with your Soldier. Fucking—'

'You're being a cunt,' she says.

'Bet you're liking this. Fysh finally out of my way?'

'No,' she says. 'That's not true.'

'You fucking hated him—always have. Why'd you even come here today?'

No hesitation. 'For you.'

'But not for Fysh?'

She shakes her head. Birdee's no liar. Says how things really are. Rare, like rocking-horse shit.

I clear my throat. 'He meant—'

'I know,' she says. 'First time I saw you together.'

Two of us tangled up. 'Hurts, I say.

Birdee nods.

Can't sit here any longer. On the pavement, I light a cigarette so my hands have something to do. My black trousers are too tight; beneath the belt the button undone. I keep pulling up my fly. I don't have a suit jacket, though my coat is dark enough to be decent. Birdee says, 'If we do this—we stay at the back.'

'Alright,' I say.

Because I came here to find out why death follows me, I don't give a fuck who's watching. I walk down the aisle while the congregation sing a hymn I've not heard before. Fysh's coffin is where it should be. But how can it be closed? There's a carpet of white flowers placed across the surface, knitted together to make the word *Brother*. Over my right shoulder, Doug's missus has hold of his arm. Can't hear what she's saying, but I have a pretty good idea. Fuck him.

I stand alone.

I am a boy in another church, trapped between Birdee and our old man. Doing my best not to bawl. Cold's come inside, and I'm sat on my palms to keep warm. Before, my old man leans in, his breath thick with cigarettes, tells me, 'Take you fucking hands out your pockets.'

Praying disagrees with me. I'd sooner something else inside my head. I think about being marooned in our apple tree with Birdee. Ladder fallen, I'm waving the saw around like a pirate. Mum is dancing in circles around us. Where are you, I wonder?

After her funeral, he leaves us on the riverbank, leans out the car window, says, 'Get yourself something to eat.' Drives away down the track, and we go inside the house.

Darker here. More than a lack of light. There are noises the house made that I can't hear any more. At first I think I've imagined them. We run room to room, listening. But Birdee doesn't hear her either. Drives us outside, where she has us holding hands. Might be because she's afraid I'll get lost too. Been months since we found Mum out on the marsh. My old man reckons not much stands still here for long. Tide and wind can turn the marsh about, rubbing away the place ground ends and water rolls in. Making mirrored pools appear where they didn't before, bursting with sky. He says she lost her way in the shifting. My old man is a liar.

'What we doing?' I say.

'Looking—' Birdee says.

'For what?'

'Know when I find it.'

'Alright—' Truth is, I know what Birdee's looking for. Maybe Mum is the grass turned purple all about us—

*

Chucked out of church. I don't bother fighting them. Cunts. Birdee was right. And I don't want to have her tell me so. I get back in the Mini, reverse down Pilot Street rather than drive past the church entrance. I know where I need to be.

I park the car on Portland Street and walk the distance to the Bus Cafe. The rain-slick pavement hums with colliding colours that's really the traffic racing by.

Inside, Hold-Your-Horses is easy to find. Blond buzz cut. I sit down opposite.

'Jesus. What the crap happened to you?'

'Alright?' I say.

'Yeah— But your face looks pretty fucked up.'

'It's nothing. Got my car—not parked far from here. You wanna go to your place?' I'm loud, and I don't care. Drunk on anger.

'Can't, mate. Not my place.'

I don't care why. 'Where then?'

'The Gates?'

'Alright,' I say. 'Let's go.'

Outside, he asks, 'What you all dressed up for?'

'Job interview.'

'Yeah—whereabouts?'

'Don't matter, mate. Didn't get it.'

'Sorry,' he says. 'You need cheering up, then?'

'Yeah,' I say. 'Something like that.'

'What about what you said the other day?'

'I was messing with you.'

'Okay—' he says.

Trailing alongside me, smoking while we walk the length of London Road, all Hold-Your-Horses can talk about is a fight in the White Hart last night. Says, 'You shoulda been there.'

Across from the South Gates is a dark gap in the wall we head towards. Down a flight of narrow stone steps, we are in the toilets beneath the road above. The floor and walls are chequered with white-and-green tiles. I'm relieved the mirrors I face are broken. The reflection thrown back belongs to neither of us alone. Instead, we resemble two people blown apart and put back together hastily. The five terrible stalls, doors ajar, are riddled with graffiti. *Do you spit. Or do you swallow.* There's a filthy urinal running the length. We are alone. Hold-Your-Horses already has his dick out, hard and pale in his hand. My own dick isn't even a little bit curious. Why'd you come here?

I came here to get fucked in the arse. While across town Fysh is beneath a heavy lid, stupid flowers keeping the light out. You're already fucked. 'I have to go,' I say. At the top of the stairs, on the pavement, I suck in deep lungfuls of air, even if it's ruined with traffic.

Hold-Your-Horses has followed me up. 'What's wrong, mate?' He puts his hand on my shoulder, and I can see his trousers are still open.

'Fuck off.' And I start walking along London Road, back towards where I parked the car.

Death has found me. The land is sick with death. This death is marsh beneath my nails, damp wind hounding my skin, doing its best to get inside. There's no shelter. Or anything left to figure out here. The whale was right. Death is everywhere—

The river is noisy, a threatening brown muddy tongue, yipping at the banks. Always biting, pushing me, relentless. I've come home to the house at the Point. Won't be long inside. Nothing much to collect. Clothes, and a picture of Fysh I keep tucked in a t-shirt two sizes too small. I'm leaving this place. Birdee has to forgive me. My old man won't care either way.

By the time I unlock the back door the telephone has stopped ringing. I guzzle down milk from the carton, not caring it's running down my chin. The ringing begins again.

'What?' I shout, hearing the water swooshing and gurgling.

I bust out of the house. The riverbank has a sly look about it, and the river is a dark line taunting me. I fucking dare you—

The river speaks to me. It says my name. Swoosh, running, snapping—

I'm here, I say. You called and I came. What—now?

The river stills some, stretches out, says, Calm down— Listen—

I am fucking listening. Just tell me what you want.

Water sounds deep, distant, like my ear is pressed up against the door of our washing machine. Don't leave. Swoosh— Swoosh— Churning—

Why the hell not? I say. You can't make me stay.

What about Hold-Your-Horses? it says.

What about him? I say.

You were mean to him before, the water gurgles. You should have let him fuck you. He wanted to be inside—

You called me out here for this. To talk about Hold-Your-Horses and his dick? Stupid— Stupid— I say. I'm leaving.

Careful, it says.

Or what? I snap.

You're not listening, the water says. I don't care about Hold-Your-Horses.

What the hell do you care about, then?

Why you were mean, it says. He was going to fuck you like you wanted. Isn't that what you wanted? To get fucked in that stinking toilet while Fysh is lying in the dark? Coward.

What'd you call me? I'll fucking kill you— You cunt river.

River roars in my ears, I'm fucking warning you, it says. Too far—

So what, I say. You always go too far. I didn't ask for this. None of it.

You asked for all it, it says, taunting me. Snap—Snapping— No I didn't, I say.

All right— If you say so, it says lapping—

I fucking hate you. I'm leaving for good, I say. You can't make me stay. It's over—

And Birdee—

Don't fucking say her name. Leave her alone.

Water laughing at me hurts my ears. The one-armed Soldier won't leave her alone.

What do you know about it? I ask.

River says, Everything—

Bollocks, I say. I will leave here.

No you won't— Swoosh— Swoosh— Coward—

I will burn the river dry, before I leave this place behind. Call what slurs beneath up to the shiny surface, and not squander my chance to wreck it. Brings me here on the mudflats, with a red can of petrol, walking an angry line. Waiting for the river to speak to me again. My black shoes are muddy. I don't know where I left my coat. This white shirt belongs to my old man and I can smell him in the wind, even though my nose is sore and running with snot. Answer me—

She says my name from somewhere behind. 'Huh?' When I turn around, her face is wind-worn, hair everywhere. There's trouble in her being here, this day of all days. 'Dora—'

'What are you doing?' she asks.

She must think me mad. Or fucked up on something. My mouth hangs open, waiting for the right thing to tell her. How can I explain the truth of this situation? That my balls ache absolutely. It occurs to me, I could pour the stinking petrol over my head, just like Doug did, set light to myself.

Roll about on the bank howling and blazing until I'm dark like dirt, and soft enough to pummel into the ground. Then the wet wouldn't have me. It'd be over. Maybe I am gutless. 'What'd you want?'

'I've not come to fight,' she says.

Then why the hell are you here? Her lips are the same shade of red as the petrol can. Taunting me. 'Alright,' I say.

She looks over at the river, eyes searching for something. 'Fysh tell you I'm pregnant?'

'He told me,' I say. Everything I didn't want to hear. 'You're keeping it, then?'

'I am,' she says, but she doesn't believe it either. 'It's why I'm here—'

'How'd you mean?'

'I need money.' Dora doesn't mess around.

I want to tell her the money in my pocket is mine. That when she clears off I'm going to fill up the Mini, keep going until the road runs out. 'You and me both,' I say. 'I only meant—' and don't bother to finish.

'You owe me—' she says.

'You should go.'

'I'm not leaving until you've heard me out.'

I believe her, too. 'Alright,' I say. 'Come on.'

'You leaving the petrol there?'

Fuck. I pick up the can. 'Best not.' The river will have to wait until I'm done with Dora. This big mess.

We're walking across the bank, pretending the wind blowing in off the Outer Roads is making it hard to talk. Truth is, I don't know what to say to this woman walking alongside me, weather knocking us together. Or what she wants to hear from me. Nothing I say can make it right. There's too much space between us.

'You go ahead,' I tell her. 'I'll put this in the shed.'

If I stay inside the shed, would she come look for me, or just go away? I leave the petrol can on the old man's workbench, where I find my coat, balled up like a stray cat.

Outside the back door, tucked up against the step, is a worn suitcase, the colour of trouble. Three feet over, a pair of polished carrion beetles are busy burying a mouse. The carcase is no longer furry, but bald like a limp dick. I'm wondering how many beetles it would take to bury a man. Rattled, I leave them to it, kick the back door closed with my foot. This is all I need.

Dora's taken off her coat because she means business. She's dressed dark as a storm. 'Didn't see you—in church,' I say.

'I was there,' she says. 'For all the good it did me. A fucking widow. At my age.'

'What'd you have me do about it? I had to go. To see him—'

'Doubt Doug saw it that way.'

'I don't give a fuck what he thinks. Besides—they threw me out.' I didn't get to see his face. Tell him anything that matters.

'I know.' She picks at a piece of hair on her cheek. 'You smarten up.'

Now I get why they call it small talk. It doesn't mean anything. It's easy for me to behave badly. 'Get on with it, then—'

'Fuck you. You can't know— I have to leave here.'

'And go where?' I say. 'You seemed alright before.'

'You're joking me?'

'I wasn't.' Nothing makes sense. Fysh is dead. Dora could just go home. 'What about the flat?'

Dora might start crying by the look of it. 'Doug's— locked me out.'

Twat. 'Can he do that?'

'He can do whatever he wants,' she nods. 'Doug owns it.'

Fysh and his secrets. I need to leave now. Get in the car. 'How about your brother?'

Dora looks at me like I'm a cunt.

'I wish it wasn't the way it is.'

'If wishes were horses,' she says.

'Look— I can't help you.' I'm leaving this place today. I plan on vanishing.

'What the fuck am I meant to do?'

'Fuck knows.' Can't be my problem. What's she expect me to do? I don't know anything about this pregnant woman standing in my kitchen. How could she bear to be around me? This is fucked up. She needs to go back to the lad in the purple t-shirt. He'll take care of her, and the baby. 'What about—'

'You owe me—you and fucking Fysh. Leaving me homeless—pregnant.'

She's right. This is my fault. If I hadn't come back here. But I did. And all I can think about is Fysh and him grinning in his green underpants, wanting everything all at once. Me. To be a father. To find Dora. Outmanoeuvre the tides themselves. This trick he intended to pull off. Bet Fysh is loving this mess. You complete bastard. 'Listen—' I say.

'Give me the money I need,' she says. 'And I'm gone. You won't see me again—'

I can't betray Fysh. He would hate me for helping his hope get away. Out of my back pocket I take a packet of cigarettes and a plastic lighter. It calms me, sucking in a lungful of blue smoke. On the exhale I think about what the hell to do. Dora is watching me, waiting, and I toss the cigarette in the sink, go back outside and pick up her suitcase, bring it indoors, say, 'The spare room's fucked up. It'll need cleaning. Stay here—'

'With you?'

'For now,' I say. 'Until I can get you the money you need.'

'No,' she says.

'Then go back to that shithole on London Road.'

'Fuck.'

'You want to see the room—or what?'

Upstairs, I show Dora the spare room, tell her, 'My room's across the hall. Bathroom's all the way at the end, next to my old man's room.' I talk quickly because I don't want her to start asking questions about Fysh. My head already aches like a bastard. 'What you got in here?' I ask, arm aching with the load of her suitcase.

'Everything I own.'

'I didn't mean anything by it,' and crack open the window. 'I'll get you some sheets.'

There's a cupboard in the hall jammed up with bedding, blankets and stacks of yellowed newspapers. When I come back, Dora is leaning against the wardrobe, eyes closed. I cough. 'Ain't that bad, is it?'

'No,' she says and it doesn't sound like a lie.

'You want anything else, I'll be downstairs.'

'This your sister's room? Wallpaper's pretty.'

'Nah,' I say. 'Birdee's room's at the top of the stairs.'

When I open my eyes, I think they can't really be open. Coal black. I do my best to rub the tar away, though it doesn't make a difference. My chest is jar-tight. Bad sounds I'm not familiar with pick at my nerves. Reaching around for the old man's rifle starts my heart hammering. What the fuck is happening? Where the hell did I leave the rifle? Fucking think. Doug is here. He wants me to know it, to shit my underpants. He's in the kitchen. Closer now. Hallway. Outside this room. I bet he isn't alone. Gutless cunt. A rectangle of light, like a tipped television, and her voice, 'You okay?'

Idiot, I tell myself. Stupid.

Dora puts on the light, making me squint. 'I've made us something to eat.'

'Alright' I say.

In the bathroom I lean against the door. Watch the bare bulb. Catch my breath. Wait for the pain in my chest to drop away. Then I flush the toilet, even though I didn't really need to piss. On the way past my bedroom I tuck my old man's rifle inside.

When I come into the kitchen, Dora says, 'Nothing special.'

The table is set with knives and forks, and a knackered bottle of ketchup in the middle. She's folded kitchen roll into neat triangles, one apiece. There's a can of beer, going flat, and she has a glass of cloudy water. This must be what's it's like to be married. Smells like the Bus Cafe in here. 'Looks good.'

Dora doesn't believe me.

'Hospital telephoned,' she says. 'Your dad needs picking up in the morning.'

'Alright.'

'How sick is he?'

'Can't be that bad if they're sending him home,' and I shovel a heap of Dora's cooking into my mouth, wishing right away that I hadn't.

'Called my boss this afternoon,' she says.

'What for?' I ask.

'See if I could get my old job back.'

'Did you?'

'I can start tomorrow, two days a week. Miserable twat.'

'Money'll be useful, though.'

'Better than nothing.'

'Don't worry,' I tell her. 'I haven't forgotten our deal,' and take a swig from my can. These tins she tipped into the saucepan to heat up taste like dog food. 'What's wrong?'

'Your dad—what will you tell him?'

'That I'm helping you out—after Fysh.'

'And are you?' she asks.

'Soon find out,' I say.

From up on the roof I can see the fishing trawlers, dots of colour cutting their way through the muddy tidewater, heading for the Outer Roads, or maybe Lynn Deeps. Then behind me the docks, cranes scraping the low-lying cloud.

Sometimes clouds don't look light to me. Instead, like slabs of wet concrete that any moment could drop from the sky and flatten the house. I'm up here fixing the aerial now the wind's turned itself around, blasting some other place. Then I'll head out to the hospital. I've told Dora I'll drop her off at the launderette, where she takes care of the coin-operated washing machines and dryers. I don't know what my old man will have to say. But I won't ask him for the money to pay off Dora.

From here the river looks still. I flick the dog-end into the air and start climbing down the ladder. Wondering where to get Dora's money from. Then we can both get out of here.

At this hour the kitchen is not mine alone. The early grey light seeping through the window is stark against my old man's profile. So that he looks like a sheet of flat iron. His breath is awkward, rattling on the exhale. Smoke from his cigarette strays from where his hand is resting on the black table. 'Sit down,' he says.

I put myself in the chair opposite. Don't care that I'm wearing damp underpants and smell bad. The balled-up sheet rolls off my lap onto the floor beside my feet. His spare hand sparks the lighter, looks like a goldfish darting beneath the surface. For a flash I'm a boy again, and he is saying, You scared the fuck out of me.

'You've wet the bed?' he says.

I nod.

'Thought you'd sneak it past me?'

'Dunno.'

'Dora does plenty around the place without extra from

you.' He smokes, says, 'Reckon you've caused her enough trouble already.'

Easy to see where this is going. Dora's charmed him. He's reminded me every day this past month that I've ruined her life. 'Dora knew what she was marrying,' I say.

'Did she?' And now he's coughing madly, the kind that takes its time before dying down.

I wait, watching dawn break behind him. Though I wouldn't care if he never spoke another word.

Then, clear as anything, he says, 'You remember that fish you hid beneath your bed?'

I do. 'The pike.' It lay shiny inside the wooden first-aid box. My big secret.

'There's your trouble.'

'I don't understand.'

'These things you want. That dead pike. Tim Fysh. Your sister—'

'What about them?' I say.

'They can't ever be right.'

What the hell does he know? 'What's it matter to you?'

'Matters that you do right by Dora.'

'I'll get her bloody money.'

'You'll get no help from me.'

I hate every bit of his guts. 'Why—' my voice is small, like I'm still on the edge of the in-between place, where the whale now lives. 'Why'd you hate me?'

He grunts. 'No use trying to tell you anything. Never has been,' he says to himself.

'I want to know.'

'Don't be an idiot.'

'Just fucking tell me—'

'Careful,' he says. 'Go get yourself cleaned up. I need you to go into town. Pick up my prescription.'

'That day at the lake. Why'd I scare you? What did it matter if I made it out the water?'

He looks up at the ceiling. He won't find anything there. Just leftovers, smoke and hard chip oil.

'We're done talking.'

'But—'

'I mean it,' he shouts.

I pick up the sheet, stuff it in the washing machine. My old man's gaze feels like a bullet in my back. Real enough to imagine hot blood running, pooling in the crack of my arse. Maybe I should sit back down. Tell him everything I've never been brave enough to say. Still I can't.

Upstairs I run both taps together. Climb into the bathtub wearing my dirty underpants. Fuck him. And I punch the wall. Doesn't hurt. The crack in the tile is pleasing beneath my fingertip. I'm tempted to smash up the lot. Until there's nothing left but the plaster beneath.

Stupid, but when Fysh calls and says to get myself into town, he's something big to show me, I thought maybe he'd got a trawler of his own. 'Nah, mate,' he says. 'That comes after. First—this place,' opens up his arms wide, like he's beneath the big top taming lions. We're standing inside his new flat. Though there's nothing new about it. 'Come look.' And I'm pulled outside onto his wet concrete balcony. There's a plastic chair with three legs and an orange traffic cone. We both know it stinks out here. And the view is rubbish, rain hitting hard now. But it beats his bedroom at home with Doug. 'What'd you reckon?'

'It's pissing it down,' I say.

'Nah, about—'

I bump his shoulder, messing with him. 'Looks alright.'

'Finally,' he says, 'Place of my own.'

Fysh is not wrong. Be nice to have someplace safe to fuck. There's always somebody to be bothered about. My old man. His brother. 'Bet Doug's glad to be rid of you?'

'He reckons now I'm nineteen he'd have booted me out anyway.'

Sounds like Doug. Fysh moved in with Doug after their mum's boyfriend beat the crap out him. Banged up his face pretty good. Fysh never talks about her. Believes she's no good. But I reckon it might be because their old man drowned when they were little and she can't stand being reminded. Memory is hard like that.

Before I've any say, Fysh has me in his spare overalls hammering hard against the bathroom wall. There's pieces of tile all over the place.

Every time I take a break, we hear a fist thumping behind the wall. 'Fuck you,' Fysh yells again. His red hair appears cloudy.

'Call it a day?' I ask.

'How about,' he says, tugging his overalls down, 'we go to the Greenland?'

'Alright.'

We're laughing while we hustle into the Greenland, wondering if the wet will turn his hair hard with plaster. 'I'll get the beers,' Fysh says.

I watch him at the bar; above his head a giant jawbone looks like it might eat him up. Belongs to a whale and has been there ages.

When Fysh comes over, his hands full of beer, he says, 'That's the girl I told you about. Name's Dora.'

I don't care about the pretty girl at the bar.

'Reckon I'll marry her.'

'You pissed already?'

'Nah,' he says. 'We should go to the off-licence afterwards.'

'Why?'

'Get some cans. Go back to my place. Celebrate.'

His place. Sounds good. 'Alright,' I say, glancing back over my shoulder, wondering why my balls ache all of a sudden.

The river speaks to me. Crybaby, it says.

Fuck off, I tell it.

Your old man thinks you're a gutless little queer. A big crybaby. You wet the bed—again. Dirty little—

I drank too much beer. That's all, I shout. It could happen to anyone.

I don't believe you. Liar—

Who cares what you think, anyway?

Water says, The whale does.

Go away.

Your old man does. And he's right. Want—Want—Want—

He's a cunt. And he doesn't know nothing.

He knows Dora.

No, he doesn't—she's tricked him.

Water whirls, You hate her?

She's too hard to look at.

Water thinking about things sounds like cold bathwater draining away.

Crybaby, it gurgles. He hates you.

I don't care about him. I want—

What do you want? water asks.

Quiet— I want you to shut the fuck up. For you to go away.

Water rushes into my ears, Hate— Hate— Hate—

Dora is not like other women. Least unlike any I've ever known. Though there haven't been too many. At first I figure the old man is keen on having her around because she's charmed him. Then I'm thinking it's plain hate. Now Birdee's off on the marsh with the Soldier, I'm all he has to punish. Because he knows having her here is tough on me. The way digging dirt in winter is, when the ground's frozen mean and the shovel won't bite. Truth is, Dora's full of surprises. I reckon that's why Fysh fell for her in the first place. And this scares me.

Some days it's hard to look at her. Willing a way out of this situation. Makes me uncomfortable, knowing she can see past my t-shirt to what's buried beneath my skin, gathering there. Agitated, I am reminded that I have to do right by her. Get the money she needs to take off for good. Times like this I close my eyes, lids are lead-heavy. The very sight of her ruining my view.

Now Dora's tapping on the kitchen window, beckoning

me indoors. I'd bark like a dog if it wouldn't make things worse.

'Where've you been all day?' she asks, working hard to swallow her anger. Even mad she's pretty.

'Pills.' And I put the old man's prescription drugs on the tabletop.

'He said you left right early.'

'That's right.' I offer up nothing further.

'Doesn't matter now.'

'What's the trouble?' I want to know.

Dora's no fool. I've stayed away on purpose. Been at Black Barn all this while. Watching the clouds galloping across the tear in the metal roof. Smoking. My hand down the waistband of my underpants, thinking about Fysh. Tugging getting me nowhere.

'Come on,' she says.

Why'd she call me indoors to take me back out? Dora can be confusing.

Outside Dora lights up half a cigarette she must have stubbed out earlier. A couple of short drags, offers me the butt.

'Nah,' I say shaking my head.

'You'll wish you had,' she says.

'You gonna tell me what you're hacked off about?'

'Doug turned up early morning. Was hanging out the wash.'

Fuck. 'What'd he want?' Other than me dead.

'Heard I was living here.'

'Who the hell from?'

'He didn't say. He thought you were hiding inside the house. On account of the car parked here.'

'Twat.'

'Wanted to know how I could live with the man my husband was fuck—'

'I'll fucking kill him.' Dora hands me the cigarette. It's barely burning, stings my lips when I suck the last drag from it. 'That all?' I flick the dog-end to the dirt, where it dies like a dud firework.

She shakes her head, eyes bewildered. 'Told me I should get an abortion—' she says. 'I told him it's too late for that. To get fucked. That's when he grabbed hold of me—threatened to kick the baby out of me.'

'Jesus fucking Christ.' I sound like Fysh.

'Your old man came out with the rifle. Said he had no problem using it.'

'Fuck.'

'Doug took off, after that.'

'He hurt you—the baby?'

'No—I'm—we're all right. But—I had to explain things.'

My old man in a standoff with Doug would have been a big eyeful. Like outlaws on television. 'How much you tell him?'

'All of it,' she says. 'What Doug did to you—at the pit.'

'Alright,' I say. Because what does it matter now? He'll tuck it away someplace, take it out and turn it over in the palm of his hand until it doesn't puzzle him.

I leave her standing in the garden, go inside and get the car keys.

'Where you going?'

I look back over my shoulder. 'Where'd you think?' The

tide still shows signs of trawlers passing down the river, the muddy swell smacking the riverbank. I can see the cloud of gulls in the shifting light. He'll be there.

The fleet is loud and rough with fishing sounds. Trawler masts jammed up along the concrete quay. Greasy yellow light fights off dusk, rippling on the wet. There's rope tangled everywhere. Rusty winches whining under the weight of sacks rammed with shellfish. Men smoke and bark. Lads complain, eager to get home to their girlfriends. Here the air is thick with sweat and boat fuel. But the gulls don't give a damn. Soaring above the rigging, scrapping for position. They have chased the boats inland from the Outer Roads. Beneath their angry chorus the river is restless. It knows I'm here. Sniggering—

'You lookin' for someone, mate?' he says. There's an unlit cigarette behind his big red ear. He looks like an idiot.

'Don't worry yourself,' I tell him.

'Wanker,' he calls after me.

I track along the quay towards the brick shelter, weaving this way and that. Head down. Hands stuffed in my pockets, stepping over loose rope, on my way to the *Ann Marie*. Then I see him—Doug catches sight of me. Comes charging, all muscle and snout, thundering across the quay like a lunatic.

The blackness flickers, though does not linger. I am here, the in-between place. Flat on my back, I twist my head around, this way and that, looking for Fysh, any sign of his brilliant red head in the flickering half-light. Fysh—I shout—Fysh. I can't feel the ground beneath me, but it must be there, pressed against my coat, holding me. He's close by. 'Give me— '

'Give me a chance,' Fysh says. Has his hands up like a boxer, rocking. But he doesn't want to knock me out with an eight-punch combination. Instead cups my face in his rough palms. 'Sorry.'

I don't reckon the way I feel about him makes much sense. 'Alright,' I say. But how can it be? I hate this fucking brick shelter we're hiding underneath. Though the trawlers are gone. Fishing on the Outer Roads. I've come here for Fysh to tell me the way it will be afterwards. When he's a husband, day after tomorrow—

He lets me go. Taps two cigarettes from the packet, lights them up, handing me the spare. Then he leans back against the rough wall. The tide has taken the water from the quay. Stinking mud shiny with sunlight. 'How's Birdee's boat coming?'

'Not bad.' I've hauled it out of the water. Let the wood dry out.

'Bet you haven't even started—'

'I will.' Promised Birdee I'd paint it up. 'What's it matter?'

'Doesn't, I guess,' he says.

'My old man's at work,' I say, 'Come back with me.'

Fysh shakes his head. 'Can't, mate.'

There's about a billion things I want to tell him. But Fysh won't hear me. He said everything he had to say before when he pleaded for his chance. The noise of chain being guzzled up gets my attention. Across the quay two lads are running the winch at Lynn Shellfish. 'For how long?' I say.

'Huh?'

'You want me to keep away?'

Fysh flicks the dog-end onto the ground. 'Dunno,' he says. 'For good.' But I can see he doesn't mean it. 'Dunno—a while, maybe.'

There he goes complicating everything. I suck the last of the smoke from my cigarette. 'Alright.' I'll stay away. 'You should go—' Standing here alongside him hurts too much. Worse than fucking dying, I reckon.

Fysh opens his mouth. Changes his mind. Then he walks away, no turning back, towards the docks. The cranes there, glistening in the sunlight, are scraping the sky. I wish they'd pull the whole blue down. Covering everything.

'Get—the—fuck—up,' Doug shouts.

'Huh?' There's a heavy weight, sliding wet around my face. I can taste hot iron. Smell blood. I'm bleeding. Doug—

'Get up,' he yells again. 'Fucking little poofter.'

I'm yanked to standing so fast I might vomit. I can hear the lights spinning behind Doug's head, see the sounds I should be listening to. Someone has my arms pinned behind my back. Doug delivers a gut punch. Doubled over, vomit shooting out my mouth, splashing his big boots.

'Fucking hell.'

Gathered around, a gang of fisherman are wondering about this situation ahead of them. Sky at dusk is the canvas of a giant circus tent stretched out over our huddled heads. The fishermen in their yellow dungarees are noisy lions prowling. Jaws grinding. My old man told me one time two lions broke loose from the circus, killed a lad not far from here. Now it's my turn. Town paper'll read *Local Lad Mauled to Death*. Do something— 'Dora,' I say. 'Do—ra.'

'Shut the fuck up,' Doug says.

'You all know Tim Fysh's Dora?' I say.

'I won't ask again,' he warns, inching forward.

Keep going. 'She's pregnant.' Fuck you Doug, coward bastard. 'Kicks her out of her home—pregnant and all, and no husband. Tells her she should get an abortion.' Bang— Doug's fist and my chin. Misfired. And it doesn't hurt. 'Your mate here, threatened to kick the baby out of her.' It doesn't matter that they all know I'm a poofter. That I like getting fucked in the arse. Because hitting a pregnant woman is worse.

'Let him be,' a lion alongside me says.

Then another who's come out behind me from the shelter, 'Too far, mate.'

'Get going, lad.'

I don't need to be told two times. It's hard walking back down the quay to where I parked the Mini. Not because my face hurts, or the horn that's honking between my ears, but the ache in my underpants, telling of the trouble to come.

Feeling low. About as close to the ground as I'm able to be without lying down.

'Jesus Christ.' She asks, 'Was it worth it?' Dora is using kitchen roll to wipe blood and snot off my mouth and chin. I can hear my old man watching television in the other room. Uninterested.

I don't say anything. Because I can't stop myself, I cry in front of her. This is all my fucking fault.

Dora brushes my eyebrow, running her thumb back and forth, following the arch.

'Don't do that,' pushing her hand away. It's what Fysh would do.

'What's wrong?'

'Nothing.' It doesn't matter.

She sees the lie laid out before her. Gets up from the kitchen table, walks over to the sink and turns the tap to running. 'Fysh was no good.'

'Nah,' I say. 'That's not true.' I knew him longer—

P urple water cuts an unholy line through the landscape. Reckon I'm standing on the wrong side. Every day I say, Tomorrow morning I'll leave this place. But I don't get away. Or see the chance. Even tried praying. Not kneeling or nothing. Just whispering now and again. Not that it's getting me anywhere. Dora has me turning all kinds of ways. Hauling this and that, figuring I've nothing better to do. Making sure my old man's breath stays steady. Last couple of weeks the only peace and quiet I've had, sleeping on the riverbank in the long grass. Or after dark, wanking in my bedroom to night noises. Thinking about Fysh.

I can hear Dora, though I'm far enough along the track to leave her call behind, let the bank and river listen instead. Before long I'm riding down Cross Bank Road. Past shed twenty-five on Alexandra Dock, I leave Birdee's pushbike against the wall outside the office. Sign on the whitewashed window says *Hiring*. But the old cunt inside cares more about how my old man is doing. 'He's alright,' I say. Tells me to come back week after next. But I don't believe him. My name's rubbish around here and no one'll hire me. Fuck you, Doug.

Now I'm looking at the Pilot. Been boarded up for years. Round back, the path is wild with nettles. I am not alone. Two lads lean against the derelict wall, annoyed by graffiti. Further down there's an older man, could be forty, but it's hard to tell. He has a face that'll have to pay for what he's after. Doesn't matter how badly I want Dora's money. I'll not stay here. I have a mind to ride home; nothing left but ask Birdee for help.

I'm held up. Instead of heading out on the marsh to find Birdee, Dora's at the back gate. Hounding me. Says, 'You're back, then.'

'Looks like it,' I say.

'Good.'

'What's wrong?'

'Hedge needs cutting.'

It does. 'I'll do it tomorrow.'

'Told him you'd do it today.'

Fuck. 'Alright.' It'll take the rest of the afternoon.

'See you later,' she says.

Dora gets into the Mini. She has a shift at the launderette. Be gone all afternoon. I consider finding a spot on the riverbank to put my back against. The hedge behind me is wild with weeds. Then there's new branches all over the place. If it were down to me, I'd not cut a fucking leaf, leave it to grow as high as the house. That way nobody passing by on the wet would even know we're here.

*

From this spot I can see trouble chasing the last of the day-light along the track. Behind him there's a cloud of dust looking like a swarm of blackbirds harassing him. Fuck. This is all I need. Fit Lad gets off his motorbike, cutting the engine. He walks on over.

Taking hold of me in a tight hug, he says, 'Fucking missed you.'

Steady on. I am hot and sweaty from hacking the hedge all afternoon. And then we're in the wreck on the marsh, I'm on my knees, and the head of his fat dick is pushing against my tonsils. What the fuck am I doing?

It's not long before he's buttoning up his trousers, and I'm off the dirt. 'What you doing here?' I say, walking back towards the house.

'Told you already,' he says, bumping shoulders.

I can smell dinner in the breeze. Dora came home from the launderette an hour ago and is waiting for us at the back door. Leaning in such a way that she looks a little less pregnant. I want to say something smart. But I don't.

'Nice bike,' she says. What she really means is Fit Lad is handsome.

I say, 'This is_____.'

'You hungry?' she asks him.

'Starving,' Fit Lad says.

Dora is eyeballing me. 'Looks like you've eaten already.'

I turn to Fit Lad, knowing my face is lobster-hot. 'Nice one.' And flip up the bottom of my t-shirt, hoping I get his cum off my chin. This is really wrong—

*

111

Some things I see will never be right. The sperm whale lies aground on a halo of dirty blood. Trespassing. Its last spent breath hangs like sea-smoke. Tide's on the turn, and wind's galloping off the water, but I don't feel nothing with this huge wall of wet concrete before me, bruise-coloured in beach-light. Church comes to mind. The sea God's congregation, sat listening on rows and rows of green boulders, worn smooth with grace.

This whale might be God. If I believed that rubbish. Still, I hurt something terrible, like I've been kicked in the bollocks. I'd put my back to it if I thought it would make any difference. Tread up the beach until I'm just a lad sat on a rock. But the whale speaks to me—

Here I am, listening to fucked-up things that won't come loose, not even when I bash my fist against the side of my head. The ache in my balls thumping along with my heartbeat. This beast wrestling the tide to tell me— 'Nah—can't be—'

And I'm legging it. Making my way over tide-stones and plastic bottles, up concrete steps, slick with winter. Seeing some trick has turned my white trainers pink.

Fit Lad's motorbike is where I left it. Engine rumbling beneath my arse, I bust out of here, passing Thomas's Amusement's Arcade, entrance lit up in electric green. I can't shake what I heard from the dead. Taunting me. Outside O'Quigley's, a fat woman standing under a tiny red umbrella whistles when I ride by. Then onto the seafront, dodging old men who rock like skittles in the wind. The Ferris wheel is rusted still. I want to get off his motorbike, climb up to the top view, where I can look back at the line of sand, and see if I have made it up. But I don't. Because I haven't. A crowd of carrion beetles circling my whale.

Outside Ron's chip shop, Fit Lad is sheltering himself from the wet. Behind him a big glass window covered with clouds. He smokes his Benson & Hedges hurriedly, leaning like he's somewhere between horny and bored. I ease off his motorbike. Walk over. Up close, he stinks of burnt batter and yesterday's t-shirt. But I know if I lick his skin it will taste of salt and the soap he buys from the pound shop on Lincoln Street. 'Where the fuck've you been? Ron's doing his nut.'

'Nowhere,' I say.

'Told Ron I reckoned you were down on the beach. Big whale's washed up. You hear?'

'Nah,' I lie. I won't talk about that.

Fit Lad flicks the dog-end onto the pavement. 'You all right, or what?'

'I'm leaving—'

'You gone simple? Stop messing about,' he says. 'Your shift's started already.'

'Nah—this isn't a joke. We're done. I'm—' I watch him pull on the first layer of hate. 'I can't be here any more with you. It's—'

'What're you saying?'

'It's obvious.'

'You're being a twat.'

He's not wrong. 'Forget about it,' I say. Unable to stand it, turning and walking away across the green, hands tucked underneath my armpits, because there's no room left over in my trouser pockets.

*

113

Tracing circles with my finger on the chipped plaster wall. Tired and bad tempered, I want to sleep. Fit Lad is alongside me in bed. The window is wide open because the night is warm with marsh noises. He won't leave me be. Tugging at the back of my underpants, 'Fuck off—would ya?' He pushes his hard-on against the fabric hitting the crack of my asshole. 'I'm fucking serious,' I say.

'Jesus—all right,' he says, 'Fuck's sake.' Getting out of bed and putting on the lamp. I watch him pull on his underpants, the head of his dick sticking out the top. Red and shiny with bucking against me. He lights a cigarette. 'What the fuck's up with you?'

'Tired is all.' But it's not only that. Fit Lad can't be here, agitating things. Dora, my old man, it's messing me up. Guilt gnawing at my bellybutton. Hard to figure what Dora makes of Fit Lad. Me rubbing my old man's nose in it.

'Not yours is it—the baby?'

I want to punch him in the face. He's behaving like a twat. 'Nah,' I say. 'Course not. She's married. Was—'

'What—he leave her or something?'

'Something,' I say. 'Was a mate of mine.'

'Was?'

'Died, not long back.'

'Fuck. What happened?'

'Drowned,' I say.

'Fuck.' Then, 'She's nice.'

I don't much feel like talking.

'Your old man's a bit of a tosser.'

He is. 'He's dying. Asbestos.'

114

'Fuck. Sorry,' he says. 'That why you left like that?'

Because Fit Lad won't shut up, I scrunch my knees up to my chin and wiggle out of my underpants, flip over onto my belly. When he starts squirming two wet fingers inside me, I watch the broken plaster, seeing all kinds of shapes there. A bear with three legs chasing after a man.

Morning, and I'm on my back looking up at the ceiling. I can hear the river through the window. It's not loud. Sneaky cunt. Fit Lad is hard to share a bed with. He's pressed up against me. Has spit on his chin. I need to piss badly. I shake him, 'Get up.'

'What?'

'You need to leave,' I say.

'What—right now?'

'Yes.'

His eyes still closed. 'Why the fuck does it have to be right now?'

'Because the river—'

'The river wants me to leave?'

'Yes.' It's for your own good.

'You been sniffing glue, mate? Remember that twat from—' Fit Lad rolls over, pulling the sheet with him. 'Go back to sleep.'

I climb over him, out of bed. Position myself, dick in my hand, and start pissing on Fit Lad. He jumps up like a wasp stung him. 'You mental cunt. What the fuck are you doing?'

He pushes past me on his way to the bathroom. I hustle over to the window and finish my business.

Pull on some underpants and talk through the door. Explain that I was just messing about.

'Get fucked,' he says.

'Alright' I say.

Fit Lad busts open the door, 'Twat.'

I sit down on the toilet seat. My old man has stashed a packet of cigarettes and a plastic lighter behind the toilet cistern, held together with a red rubber band. He believes Dora doesn't know about it. I light one, suck in a lungful of smoke, listening to Fit Lad bang about in my bedroom. With my back against the pipe, I tip my head enough to watch the toilet chain behave like a pendulum, dowsing for shit.

Cigarette's not half smoked before I hear the engine growling. I smile, thinking about the look on Birdee's face when I tell her how I got rid of Fit Lad. It's for his own good. Everything that comes near the water ends up ruined.

The river speaks to me. Says, You're a dirty cunt.

Why'd you call me that? I ask.

Water running, gurgling, says, Fit Lad's cum messing up your face.

What about it? It's just cum. My balls are full of it.

Fysh wouldn't say so, water sliding this way and that. Cum eating—

Don't reckon he'd give a fuck, I say. What's it matter now?

Everything matters—don't you know that yet?

More stupid riddles. Enough—this is bollocks. I did what you told me. Fit Lad's gone—I sent him away.

Water washes all around. You're fucked up.

Because you're making me fucked up, I yell back.

Rippling, rolling, gathering from beneath, water says, Can you still taste him?

Leave me alone—

The water is moving faster, swooshing. He's not the whale. Even if he does taste of the sea.

I fucking know he's not the whale, I say. What're you getting at?

River says, The whale scares the fuck out of you. Don't eat it.

This is going nowhere, I say. I'm not afraid of the whale. I didn't eat it.

Liar, the water yips. Row—row—row—

Alright, I say. A bit—the whale scares me a little bit.

The water is lapping quietly, whispering, The whale is dead. Just like Fysh.

Shut up.

And your mother.

Shut the fuck up.

And Birdee.

I won't listen any more, I say. You're talking like a loon.

The river gurgles, ripples, swooshes, says, The dead are all behind you. Following you.

No—

Lined up like a row of soldiers, it says.

You mustn't say that. Don't fucking say that.

Or what? the water asks.

I'll throw myself into you—drown myself.

The river stills, a small gurgling whisper, You wouldn't dare—Joe Gunner.

The grass is everywhere. Any day now it'll turn a surprising shade of purple. As it does every year around this time. The marsh reminds me nothing's what it appears to be. Except the damn flies, all over the place. If I could peek up my own arsehole I reckon I'd find them there. Buzzing.

I'm holding hands with Birdee. There's noisy grasshoppers underfoot, and another sound I don't know the name of. We go where it takes us. I've missed her. She's been hiding out here, fucking the Soldier in his houseboat.

'You're quiet' she says. 'You want to talk about it?'

'Nah,' I say. 'I'm alright.'

She slows down. 'Out with it—'

'Reckon you could loan me some money?'

'What's it for?'

'Dora.'

'I can't.'

'Cuz—it's for her?'

'No,' Birdee says. 'I don't have any.'

'Alright,' I say. And I'm a little bit mad. But it's more than the money. Even if she does think I'm being stupid. 'Why'd you rather be with the Soldier than me?'

Birdee smiles. 'You know why.'

'Nah, I don't.'

'If Fysh were here, would you be walking with me?'

'I would.' But there'd be the pull hauling me away. It's not easy having a sister who knows everything. Makes me settle down. 'You doing alright out here—with him?'

'Yes.'

'He's good to you?'

'Can't complain.'

'You coming home soon?'

'He ever ask about me?'

My old man's a cunt. 'House isn't the same without you.'

'Fuck him—'

'He's happy having Dora around.'

'What's she like?'

'Different—'

Birdee's gone ahead now, leading the way. 'Different—how?'

'Dunno.' Dora's hard to pin down. 'She's surprising.'

'She remind you of me?'

'Some.' Yet she's not you. Sometimes I think she still hates my guts. Then she'll do something sweet. Confusing. 'Dora doesn't know me like you do.'

'How you gonna get the money?'

'Thought about selling my arsehole,' I say.

'You're fucking joking me?' she says, standing still. Hands on her hips.

'Nah, honest. But I didn't do it. I reckon it'd take a year to earn enough.'

'Close to two, I'd say.'

Here we are. Laughing and carrying on. Until we're not.

Birdee is taller than me. But only by two lines marked on the wall. We are looking at the unimaginable. Mum is nearly naked, lying on her back. Legs in the tidal creek bobbing up and down. The water, nudging, is trying to stir her up. But she won't be moved by the muddy brown wet, no matter how much it taunts her. Her face is frozen. Hair a tangled bundle of wet straw. It's hard to tell where she ends and the bleached reeds begin. She's watching the sky, a miserable stain of blue. Gaze rigid. But who knows what she's seeing?

I have pissed my shorts. Warm water pooling in my left trainer. Birdee has her palms over her ears. That's how I know I'm screaming. Like I'm on fire. One continuous roar—

'Hey—' Birdee says.

'Huh?'

'You'll figure it out.'

'What?' I ask.

'How you'll get the money.'

I shake my head. 'Not that.' I am afraid the whale—river is telling the truth. The dead are following me. 'I'm in bad trouble.'

Birdee snorts. 'Is there any other kind?'

'I dunno—what to do.'

121

'Don't do anything then,' she says, taking my hand again. 'Alright.'

Dora is wrong. She thinks I'm stupid because I made Fit Lad go away. We're in the garden, barefoot treading sharp grass. There's a white plastic basket between our feet, spilling over with tangled laundry. She's roped me into pegging while she hangs. Smells like childhood. Here I'm reminded of Mum, before my old man drove her out onto the marsh.

'Switch over,' I say.

'You're changing the subject.' She shakes her head. Stubborn like thunder flies. Holding my t-shirt on the line, I peg each end. 'Why'd he leave in such a hurry?' she asks.

'Dunno.'

'Don't be a twat.'

Fit Lad is the last thing I want to be thinking about. Only yesterday his dick was grazing my tonsils. Him saying how much he'd missed me. Wanting him to be Fysh, and not himself. Fit Lad was somebody to forget everything with.

'Heard him shouting.'

Even washed I can see dark toe-prints on these white socks I'm pegging. 'Was nothing.'

'Sounded like something. Was it about Fysh?'

'Nah.' But who I am kidding? I can't tell her getting rid of Fit Lad was what the water wanted. It was for his own good. Instead, I say, 'I did something stupid. That's all.'

'What?'

'I pissed in his face.'

Dora stops pegging. Her mouth hung like a cupboard door. 'On purpose?'

'He wouldn't get out of bed.' And because it was more than that. 'I didn't want him here.'

'Fair enough,' Dora says. 'But there's easier ways to get rid of someone.'

'Is there?' Right away I feel like an arsehole. 'He reckoned I'd been sniffing glue.'

'Can see why.'

I deserve that. 'I'm not crazy,' I tell her, using my foot to slide the basket along the ground.

'But—' Dora says, 'a lot of crazy shit happens around you.'

She's not wrong.

'You ever going to tell me—about Fysh?'

Just shake my head.

'I know how he died. But—'

Somewhere between my favourite blue t-shirt and the old man's vest, Dora has me trapped. Made it so even if I weaved in and out of these clothes all day long, chasing my own tail, I'd still be caught on a line. 'I don't believe I'm crazy.' Who's to say what crazy is anyway? 'The law found me in the river.'

'What were you doing there?'

Because it's not an unreasonable question, I say, 'Listening—' Ankle deep in muddy water, wearing just my underpants. 'To the water talking.'

'Talking?'

'It speaks to me.'

Nothing here but water swooshing, murmuring, telling me things no one has an ear for. Terrible things. And I can't say how long I've been this way, or how far time will flow before I'm out of the wet.

123

Lights whirling and the law are here. One tall. The other shorter. I am rattling with cold. The tall one is rubbing my arms with rough hands, scratching my skin. He has black eyes, like the shiny dials on the old man's radio, mesmerising. The shorter one unfolds a blue blanket, wraps it around my shoulders, covering my bare chest. They move me towards the house, one either side, shepherds herding sheep. I won't run away. There's nowhere to go.

'What's your name, son?' he asks, sitting me down on a kitchen chair.

Moving my lips, but no sound comes out. Nothing is alright.

'It's all right, son. Take your time.'

'Dunno.'

'This your house?'

'The whale did it. The whale—' I tell him.

The short one says, 'You been taking any drugs, fella?' He doesn't wait for me to answer, leaves the kitchen. I know where he's going.

'I'm not crazy,' I tell the tall one.

'Calm down, son. Was it you who called the police?'

I'm nodding.

'And this is your house?'

'My old man's.'

'Who died? You told the—'

'The whale,' I say.

'What kind of drugs have you taken?' Using his thumbs, he stretches my eyelids open. 'It's all right. Just having a look.'

The short one is back. Says something into the tall

one's ear, but I can't hear what. Tells me, 'You calm yourself down now.' And he leaves me, watched over by the other.

When he comes back downstairs, he has the same miserable look on his face. Slides out a chair for himself and sits down. Tells his mate to use the radio in the car outside.

'All right,' he says. 'That's Tim Fysh upstairs. Yes?'

'It is.'

Shakes his head. 'Hey,' he says, clicking his fingers. 'Pay attention, son.'

'You want to tell me about him?'

Standing back to back, Fysh is taller than I am, but I reckon it's because his red hair is unruly. He has a chipped front tooth. It's hard to notice unless you look at him a lot. There's a brown mole halfway along his dick that goes torpedo-shaped when he gets a hard-on. He licks his lips when he gets nervous. Taps his forehead when he forgets. He's nearly never nervous. Fysh reckons there's a dead man buried beneath Black Barn. He—

'I'm asking you to tell me what happened.'

'Dunno.' Because I don't. I tell him Fysh came over because we had a fight.

'A fight?'

'Nah—an argument.'

'Was it physical?'

He says nothing when I tell him about the bath we took together. Talking about Dora and her belly. That he fucked me until the water went cold. My aching arsehole. Drying each other off, between necking cans. Or later, the river

125

talking, calling me outside, not knowing where I'd left Fysh. Because I believed he'd be safe away from the water. Off the *Ann Marie*.

'Tim, he take any drugs?'

'Neither of us did,' I say.

He doesn't believe me. Narrow eyes, jaw rigid. He hates what I am.

I open my mouth to tell him that the whale told me this would happen—suddenly my ears are rushing with sliding water, sloshing this way and that, shushing me. Telling me to shut the fuck up. That they already think I'm crazy. Instead, I say, 'Not—Tim. His name is Fysh.'

The tall one says, 'Was—'

Dora turns away from me. I'm relieved I don't have to look at her. The back of her head is smooth and shiny, colour of wet sand. 'You weren't with him when he—'

'I wasn't there.' Least, I don't know that I was.

She's moving towards the gate, and I can't let her go. Not yet. 'I didn't mean for any of this to happen.'

'But it fucking did,' she shouts.

'Yes,' I say.

'You blame it on some fucking dead whale.'

I put myself between her and the gate, leaning onto the cool iron, hands folded across my chest. I tell her about before. Living with Fit Lad in the fish and chip shop. Hiding out there. About the morning I couldn't stand it any longer. Taking his motorbike up onto the cliff, and the dark shadow waiting there for me, calling me down to the shore. A gigantic beast that has no business being there had come to tell me terrible things. Ran itself aground, dying in a pool of blood and shit. All for me—

'You're not joking me—are you?' Dora says, and moves a fly off my face. Her fingers settling on my temple for a bit.

'It's the truth.'

There might be pity in her eyes. 'What'd the whale tell you?'

No use holding back now. 'Said I'm being followed.'

'Followed?'

'Death follows me—wherever I go.'

'You're talking crazy.'

'I can prove it,' I say. Because I can.

'Go on.'

'Look what happened to Fysh?'

'You're wrong. Fysh—was just something that happened.'

'Nah.' Because I'm not wrong.

I leave Dora standing there, considering the river.

Because I feel terrible inside, stirred to do something, anything, I take the red can of petrol from the old man's workbench in the shed. Out on the marsh I pour the stinking fuel over the old trawler wreck. Inside our initials are there, side by side. Me and Fysh.

The flames lick the hairs on my arms, making me move away. Walking back towards the house, I can feel the heat through my t-shirt. Ash will settle on the water soon enough. Tide will carry what's left to the Outer Roads and still further.

Fucking gulls squawking. Beneath closed eyelids I can tell it's morning. Light forcing its way through, red circles rolling across a blackboard. Traces of a dream struggling for purchase slip away with a yawn. The sheet beneath is damp with sweat. I don't want to get out of bed, so I roll onto my back, crack open my eyes and gaze at the ceiling. Fuzzy at first, then there's marks like train tracks cutting into old plaster. A small, abandoned station with a big sign pointing north. Hair pressed against my forehead, I'm hot. I push my hand underneath the waistband of my underpants, my dick only half interested because I'm wiggling about on this journey, stretching to see around. The tracks turn east at the light fitting before disappearing into a foot-shaped lake that's really just a sad yellow stain brought about by a missing slate on the roof.

In the bathroom I splash my face with cold water. Put deodorant over yesterday's. Brush my teeth, knowing I should take the time to shave, wash properly. My hair probably stinks of wood smoke. Skin on my arms is aggravated from the fire, patches of absent hair.

Downstairs, my old man says to me, 'You look terrible.'

Fuck you.

Dora says, 'You're gonna be late.' Places a mug of tea on the kitchen table in front of me. She's been different since I torched the trawler wreck out on the marsh. Told me ash means doing the washing over. Big deal.

Tea's cold already. But I've no nerve to tell her. 'Alright,' I say. 'Best go.'

'Finish up,' my old man says.

He doesn't mean it. His coat is zipped up. There's a bag beside the chair she packed for him last night. 'Nah. I'll get another at the hospital.'

'Suit yourself,' he says. 'The tea there tastes like crap.'

'Don't reckon you'll need your coat,' I say.

Dora surprises me by kissing the old man on the cheek. 'Be careful.'

Outside the back door he stops and hacks. Guzzling gulps of river air, he holds me off with his outstretched arm. I go wait in the car. Fuck him.

The waiting room has rows and rows of blue plastic chairs, hard on my arse. My old man hasn't said a word since he got in the car on the riverbank. I think he is afraid. But I'm not certain. There's a lad around my age sat with a man who looks like his dad. They're talking back and forth, but I can't hear what about. 'You alright?' I ask my old man.

'No,' he says. 'But what's it matter?'

Here we go.

'I'm not sleeping.'

'You need some pills?'

'I'm worried—'

'I reckon you should ask for pills.'

'About Dora.'

What about your own daughter? Instead I say, 'Dora will be alright.'

'You've a crystal ball now?' he snaps.

If I had, I'd ram it down his fucking throat. 'Guess not.'

'You could marry her—'

'Who?'

'Dora, damn it,' he says, like I'm not listening to a word he's saying.

Where'd that come from? 'Fuck me.'

'Watch your mouth.'

'Why would I want to marry Dora?'

'Baby needs a father,' he says. 'Would it be that hard?'

Shaking my head, 'Doubt Dora's in a hurry for another husband.'

'Some husband.'

'What'd you know about it?'

'Tim Fysh was a degenerate.'

My fingernails can't bite my palms. I've bitten them away. And here we are again, this place where I am unable to keep myself from him. 'I'm just like him.'

'Dora'd be good for you.'

'Didn't go so well for Fysh.' Then I lean in. 'Besides, you've changed your tune. Thought I'm fucked up.'

'Shut up,' he says.

'Wanting things I can't have.' I say.

'I was wrong.'

'You—wrong?' He's going to die right now in the fucking waiting room. 'Nah—this is fucked up—even for you.'

'Keep your voice down.'

'Nobody gives a crap.' And I'm thinking about that pike beneath my bed. 'You forgotten what else was in that box?'

'Box?' he asks.

'You know—'

'I do—how could I forget when you rub it in my damn face?'

I am a thief. Worried about wanking here in the school library, I nick page eighty-eight. Ducked down in a maze of bookshelves, coughing and ripping. Wedging the folded paper down the front of my black trousers. Leaving the library behind.

Outside, tie tied to the handlebars, hastily pedalling home to the house at the Point. River on my left. Big blue sky hanging overhead, streaked with geese flapping. All the while thinking about the secret in my underpants.

I'm out in the shed. My old man's workbench is bright with sun pouring through the window. I've unfolded the photograph. There's bare-arsed lads splashing about at the water's edge. One lad's come closer. Trodden up the bank, maybe for a better look at the camera. Brought with him a palmful of river he's trouble holding on to. Drip-dripping. His smile is grainy, from a time before now, and because it's black and white I don't reckon I'll ever tell what colour his hair is. Red, I'm hoping. Reminds me of a boy at school. Everyone calls him Fysh.

Done here. I'll keep this lad in the box beneath my bed, along with the silvered pike and a fistful of stolen cigarettes.

'Then you know what I am—'

My old man's struggling with something in is head. Hesitation clouding his eyes. 'You didn't scare the fuck out of me that day.'

'Dunno what you mean,' I say.

'At the lake—I scared myself. Because I wanted to leave you in the water. Turn around and get back in the car. Drive away.'

'Why?'

'Because I knew what you'd become.'

I am adrift.

'And I was right. You and that Fysh. Pair of fucking queers.'

'That's right,' I say. 'Me and Fysh's big fat dick. I couldn't get enough of it.'

'Get the hell out of here,' he says.

'Finally,' I say. 'We agree on something.'

On the drive home there's a picture in my mind of the Amazing Esmeralda and her crystal ball, painted on the side of a fairground lorry. Hurts too much to think about anything else.

Sunlight through the kitchen window has left a mark on the facing wall that's there for good. I'm sat looking, wondering how much time it took to bleach the pattern from the wallpaper. Light's a thief, sometimes. Why'd I not notice before?

Dora has her back to me, peeling apples at the sink.

There's a big blob of pastry on the kitchen table, flour everywhere. Hair a little bit dusted, like a ghost blew on her.

'Found these in the shed,' she says. 'Thought it might cheer you up.'

I've been miserable since my old man laid out the truth at the hospital. Hearing something out loud is not the same as knowing it inside. 'Alright,' I say. Though it's hard to care about these apples my old man's been growing his entire life.

'Think they'll keep him in long?'

'Dunno.'

'You should have stayed with him.'

'Told me to clear off.'

'You do everything he tells you to?'

Dora's being unreasonable. 'He's fucked up.'

She turns around, eyeballing me. 'He's sick.'

'Crazy, more like—thinking I'd marry you.'

'One bent husband was bad enough.'

No answer to that, so I slug cold water from my glass, watch her working. I hate that word. Bent like a nail. Bent like a turn in the road. Fucking bent—

'Sorry,' she says suddenly.

What'd I care? I push off the spot I'm leaning against, pull out a chair, and sit down at the table. 'He's always been a cunt.'

'That so?' she asks.

'It is.'

'You know what I reckon?'

'What's that?'

'The light's nice here.'

'Huh?'

'At this time of day. By the river.'

'You saying you like it here?'

'Something like that.'

This is the sound of my life. Us talking. Flies buzzing. Fridge humming.

Doug is back. The leftover apple pie we were eating for breakfast unfinished on our plates. Easy talk about things that don't matter abandoned.

I'm outside on the riverbank. Doug slams the car door behind him. Sounds like thunder clapping. He's brought his mate from the Muck Works with him. Couple of cowards. I thought we were done with this when he knocked me out on the quay before. But like flies on shit, he's here in my part of the world, shouting his big mouth off about Fysh. Laying blame in the dirt between us. Expecting me to pick it up. Fuck him. I want to say Fysh is dead because of men like him, and his old man before him. And my old man. All the men who think they know what's right. And wrong—

Doug is red-faced and breathing all over mine. 'I'm not finished with you.'

Still stupid, thinking there's something to be had from doing this. He stinks of old beer and cigarettes. 'That right?' I say.

'Before—you made me look like a cunt.'

'Wasn't hard.'

'I'm gonna beat the crap out of you.'

'You reckon?' I ask. 'Hit me again, and I'll fucking kill you.'

Doug pats his mate on the shoulder. 'You hear that. He's gonna kill me?'

'If he doesn't—I will,' Dora says, my old man's rifle pointed at Doug's chest.

'Look who it is. My brother's cunt wife.'

'Fuck you.'

'You planning on using that?'

She cocks the rifle. 'Try me.'

'Dora,' I say. 'Give it here.'

'Doug, mate, we should clear off,' his mate says, hustling back to the car.

'Now—' And she passes me the rifle. Wood feels warm.

'You cunt,' Doug growls. 'You make me wanna puke. You fucking him now my brother's dead?'

'Leave her be,' I tell him. 'She didn't do nothing.'

'You fucking walked out on him,' Doug jabs his finger in her face.

'Hey,' I yelp. 'I fucking mean it.'

'You know why I left Fysh. You want me to—'

'Shut the hell up, Dora,' Doug snaps. 'I'm warning you.'

'Threatening a pregnant woman again?'

He looks ready to bust. Like a cartoon on television. Reckon steam's about to shoot out of both ears, spinning his head like a cannonball. 'Shame it was your sister and not you.'

'Go fuck yourself,' Dora yells.

'Fucking poofter.'

My finger is on the trigger. I should just kill him. What does he mean about Birdee? Only way it will ever be over.

It's too late now. He's leaving. Walking away. We stand out on the dirt track, watching the car chuck up a cloud of dirt, until there's nothing left to see.

Birdee's eyes are big and black like pebbles, watching me. She has her hands tucked inside her coat pockets. Not because it's biting cold. Birdee doesn't want to rub the livid flush my old man's left on her cheek. Fuck him for hitting her.

He hands me the rifle. 'Your turn,' he says. 'Let's see if you shoot like a little girl.' Puts his back to me. Striding away across the frozen marsh.

I raise the rifle. Take aim at the hood of his green parka. But Birdee's beside me now, gripping the end of the rifle, pushing the metal towards the hard ground. Her expression is something new. And surprising. I don't know what it means. Or maybe she just doesn't recognise me in the early light, formless like the gleaming marsh around us.

Way Dora's looking at me makes me think about Birdee. 'Here, take it.' Handing Dora the old man's rifle. 'Use it—if he comes back.'

'Where you going?' Dora asks.

'To see Birdee,' I say.

'Birdee?'

'I'm worried about her.'

And I think the situation has troubled Dora and the baby, standing in the heat. 'You'll be alright.'

Dora nods. 'Go—'

I am agitated. What the fuck was Doug banging on

about? He doesn't know my Birdee any more than he does Dora. So why do my bollocks throb badly?

Because the tide's ebbing, I cut across the marsh, jumping the creek where it's only a few feet wide, criss-crossing throughout the tall grass. Easy to get lost in this maze. My t-shirt flapping like a tail, stuffed in the waistband of my shorts. The sun and heat are drying the shit-stinking mud off my trainers and legs.

Then I'm up against it. The creek here too wide to cross, mud like quicksand. I reckon the river has tricked me. I'll need to turn around, track back a way, bear closer to the river proper. But I don't. I stand still, breathless. I have an itch that needs scratching. I call on the river—

The river speaks to me. It says, Go away—

What'd you mean? I say.

The water glides coolly beneath the muddy surface, sliding away from me. Further and further. Come back. Talk to me. Fucking—

Doug Fysh, it says, slipping back to me. Then, He's nothing like his brother.

No, he's not, I agree. He's a cunt.

The water asks, What will you do about it?

You tell me, I say. It's why I called you.

Why don't you ask Birdee?

I will, I say. When I see her. She's with the Soldier. But you already know that.

The wet is stealthy, barely making any noise at all.

You still there? I ask.

Yes, the water says.

Doug will need dealing with. Maybe I should just fucking kill him. Better for everyone, I say.

Better for Birdee. Have you asked her what to do?

I'm on my way. Like I said—she's with the Soldier.

You sure about that?

I say, Why we back here again? Around and around—

Because of Doug.

I should kill him, I say.

What did Doug say about—Birdee?

Say?

Yes.

He—

Go on—

Birdee is—

Say it—

I'm not saying another fucking thing. You hear me?

My old man calls it the borrowed hour. Time of day when the last light thrown off the winding water smudges the marshland until everything shines. Won't last long before the bright view will slip out of focus, into shadow. I'm crouching in the tall, scorched grass, watching. A big shiny beetle crawls across my hand, bothering me.

From here I can see the dark stain on the landscape that is the Soldier's houseboat. Charred black but not from fire. There's a row of t-shirts and underpants that used to be white. They're strung on a bright blue rope that stretches from the rooftop to a pole beside the tidal creek, with no breeze to move them. The Soldier stands necking a can. I don't see Birdee. Looks like the fucking river was telling the truth. Water gets everywhere, knows everything.

Without warning, the Soldier turns about, head tipped back, like a bear tasting the wind. I've not seen a brown bear before, but my old man reckoned when he was a boy, the Mart rolled into town with Oskar the dancing bear.

A big sight. Hopping from one hind paw to the other. Clever.

The Soldier's not really a bear. Even so, I've no desire to bother him. Being here feels like trouble. And Birdee's not around. Where are you?

Mostly I smoke. Sometimes my voice sounds unfamiliar in my own ears after half a packet. I'm not myself. Can't even be certain what day of the week it is. Hot days do that. They're different from every other day. Because the light comes early and goes late, hours track back and forth without a clear line, disrupting the marsh.

Hiding out in my bedroom reminds me of Fit Lad. Chip shop beneath our bedsit. Twats scrapping on the greasy pavement outside. Two of us tangled up in each other's sweat, watching rubbish on the television with the volume down. Not bothering to shower because we'll be dirty again too fast in the summer heat. Those first times when Fit Lad was unfamiliar and made small noises seemed like following a map. Figuring out when to stay on the road, when to turn off. Navigating the space between his bellybutton and the crack of his arse. Then later, not caring. Wanting him to be hasty, because it felt better to hurt than to feel nothing at all.

The same heat has followed me here. I'm thinking about Birdee. The Soldier. Dora. Ever since Doug and his mate showed up, Dora has been acting wrong. There's something on her mind. She wears it in her eyes at the kitchen table. They're big, but not with fear. It's something else. I've seen it before, with Fysh.

Downstairs in the kitchen. 'Alright,' I say, taking a glass from the draining board and pouring myself some cloudy water.

'You stink like an ashtray,' Dora says. 'Here,' handing me a clean t-shirt from the stack she's just done folding. 'You pick him up like that and he'll be—'

'Disappointed anyway,' I say, pulling off my grubby one. 'Thanks.' I don't want to go get the old man from the hospital. If it were up to me, I'd leave him there. Rotting.

'You going already? It's early still.'

'Have somewhere I need to go first.'

'Not—Doug?'

'Nah, a mate of mine,' I say.

'Don't worry about Doug,' she says. 'He's not coming back.'

Seems like Dora can take care of herself. 'I won't,' I tell her. But it doesn't matter which way I look at the situation, it still winds up upside down.

Driving into town, everyone messing with my head all at once, I pick one thing to shut down the racket. Hold-Your-Horses. Finding him won't be hard.

Instead of going inside the Bus Cafe, I tap on the big windowpane. When he looks up, he's pleased to see me. His smile, easily bored, rubs away before long. He's trying to figure out what I'm doing here.

'Hey stranger,' he says, leaning next to me on the wall outside. We're like two lizards baking our blood. Passes me half a cigarette. 'Thought you'd fucked off outta town again?'

'Nah,' I say. 'Been occupied.' Taking a drag.

'Your face looks better.'

I palm the sweat on my forehead into my hair. 'You alright, then?'

'No, mate. You gotta short memory.'

'Huh?'

'Last time I saw you—all dressed up—shirt-and-tie job.'

Fuck. That was ages ago. Day of Fysh's funeral, when I'd lied about being at a job interview. 'Sorry about that.'

'Forget about it,' he says. 'Lucky you found me here—today.'

'How come?'

'Working at the wood yard—three days a week.'

He's moved down the wall, nudging elbows. Anyway—'

'Anyway?' he asks, turning his head towards me.

Tossing the dog-end on the floor, I say, 'You up for it?'

He answers by pushing his hand down the front of my shorts, teasing my bollocks. His palm is hot, and rough from hauling planks. I'm hard now. And don't care that anyone might see us. Some days are bolder than others, I reckon.

We don't talk about where to go. Instead we ease around the town centre, not saying much about anything. Ahead of us there's a big green piece of park, and off to the right a wooden bandstand fucked up with graffiti and beer cans. I wonder if I got down on the round floor and pressed my ear against the planks I could hear a trace of something the band left behind. Like sea in a shell?

Past here, where the trees are thick with age, are the Walks toilets. Outside, a skinny lad in a blue baseball cap lights two cigarettes. He hands the spare to a girl pushing their baby.

The glow inside the stall is pouring through a skylight, chucking fat drops of sunlight onto Hold-Your-Horses' head, sliding about like wet paint. He's doing his best to wiggle his tongue into my mouth, and I can taste the can of Tango he had earlier. Hot orange. If I close my eyes, kissing him is not bad.

My dick's eager. He turns himself about, tugs his shorts down enough so I can get to the crack of his arse. Tattoos wrap around his elbows like fishing net. I spit onto my fingers. Add a layer of slick to his sweaty arsehole. I'm not careful, bucked up against him. He makes small yelping noises that speed me up, rattling the ruined toilet wall. His tan neck is lobster-hot. The place where his cropped hair first grows pricks the tip of my nose. Smell here reminds me of tinned ham. It doesn't matter, because now I'm cumming and trembling all at once.

I'm still behind Hold-Your-Horses when I hear him messing up the wall himself. 'Fuck—yes,' he groans. 'Fuck—'

I crack open the stall, stick my head out, take a look around. 'When you're done fucking about, mate—'

He yanks up his shorts. 'What's up?'

The lazy tap is spilling warm water, and it's tricky getting my dick under the flow. 'Just watch the fucking door. I've got your shit on me.'

'Fuck,' he says, not giving one.

The old man is a liar. Nurse Anthony says he isn't going anywhere, anytime soon. The ward is baked with disturbing smells. He says, 'Looks like you've had that t-shirt on all week.'

'Clean on this morning,' I tell him, hoping there's no dry cum.

'And Dora?'

'She's alright.' I won't say she misses him. 'Why'd you call?'

He leans into me. 'His name's Big Al. Doctor says he'll be dead by the morning.'

In the bay opposite, Big Al is sucking down Tizer through a plastic straw his daughter is holding. Her ponytail shakes in disbelief. When I get up for some water, she stops me. Wants to know if I'll witness the will her boyfriend got from the newsagent's for under a tenner. I tell her I'll do it. Even though I don't want to.

'What'd she want?' my old man asks.

'Nothing—don't worry about it.' We're watching Nurse Anthony closing the blue curtains around Big Al's bed. He's talking rubbish. Telling another nurse about his botched tattoo. Says it's a skeleton riding a horse through the desert, looking like it's just messed up a load of stuff. He's a twat. Big Al is busy dying. And I want to leave. 'What am I doing here?'

'I need to tell you something.'

'Huh?' I say, bothered by Nurse Anthony.

'You listening to me?'

'I am,' I tell him. 'But I won't have you bang on about me marrying Dora.'

'You won't listen to me. Maybe you'll hear Dora.'

I reckon he's fucked up on prescription drugs. 'What?'

'Dora knows about Birdee.'

Talking in tongues. More fucking riddles. 'Nothing to say about Birdee—'

146

'Listen to Dora—'

'Alright.' Because it's easier than wrestling with him.

My balls ache. I smell really bad. The old man's insane. I want to lie in a cool bath and smoke cigarettes, one after another. That's why I tell Dora this isn't a good time. She's carrying on. 'Nah,' I say. 'Later.'

'You need to see this.'

'Alright.' And the ache thumps in my underpants. Boom— Dora is standing outside Birdee's room. Boom— The door is cracked open, a big mouth waiting to swallow me up.

I'm inside the room. The whale. Both.

Drip-drip-dripping. Leaking a sad tune I don't recognise. Ink-black and airless. Dog-wet nose, raw, stinging with the stench of mud and sea. Can't tell if my eyes are screwed shut or open. Or where the small whisper is coming from. I reckon deep inside the whale's belly. So far away that maybe I have conjured it myself. A trick. Turning around and around. There it is again. Louder, sticky with travelling miles of slippery guts, scrapping for purchase. Now behind my left ear. Saying my name. Breath that teases me. Warm and sweet. It's her—Birdee. Around and around. Wrapped up in the darkness. No way to unfold it. Where'd you go? And I've disturbed this beast. Hard-metal muscle knows I'm here. Trespassing. Bleached bone readies itself, rocking me off my feet. And I need to get back up. To move. It's too late. I'm swept up in a swirl of biting-cold water messed up with fish guts. Numbing my fingers and toes. My bollocks.

Spinning me. Faster and faster, until I'm chucked up into the white.

First, because I don't know what else to do, I stand and bawl. I cry hard. Snot and water everywhere. Dora is by my side. I did this. Took the furniture from here. Ripped the carpet from the floor. Pulled down the patterned paper. Until there was nothing left to taunt me. I tore Birdee away. Burned her memory in the oil drum outside. Watched the ash rain like snow over the house at the Point. In this terrible place, I lift up my t-shirt and wipe my eyes. There's nothing here but the two of us. No whale. No Birdee. Just me and Dora in my sister's empty room.

'Everyone knows about Birdee and the lido,' Dora says.

She's watching me hard. Trying to see what's whirling behind my eyes. Last two years rushing in.

'Birdee—drowned.'

I nod.

'And you left.'

I reckon certain words are unutterable together. Just too fucked up to say. Like the word dead. And sister. Too close together. But the ache in my balls ebbs like the tide. And I'm still enough to tell the truth. 'You're dead—Birdee.'

T he river is quiet—
         Birdee's dead, I say. But you already know that.
         Water lapping against the riverbank.
Is it over? I ask.
There's nothing but river noises. Drifting near and far.
Dora reckons I should go see where she—drowned.
Flies buzzing this way and that.
I told her I don't see the point in it. Maybe—maybe not,
she reckons.
The river wants nothing from me. Lapping in and out.
But I'll go see anyway, I say. To not be afraid—

The signpost on the bank says, *No Swimming. No Diving.* Still, a pack of red-skinned lads, one bare-arsed, are splashing about and slam-dunking each other. Taking turns, they're climbing a big concrete post. Hurling themselves into the air, disappearing beneath the shiny surface head first. Bare arse has a spotty back. Livid little volcanoes, erupting down his spine, spewing onto his backside.

Their empty beer cans lay cast about like metal rocks. Sun, busting everywhere, is bleaching the blue stain from the water. I move off to their left, find a spot on the corrugated fence that isn't too hot to lean against. Behind me the lido has dried up. Where there used to be river water, now just rubbish and dog shit. Been closed down since Birdee died.

I sit here smoking, watch the back of a one-armed man. The Soldier. He's wearing a dirty white t-shirt ruined with sweat. 'Stupid cunts,' he says, looking back over his shoulder.

'Huh,' I say, sliding down the concrete slab, a little bit closer, grazing my pockets.

'They deserve to get fucked up.'

He has a week's worth of black beard, eyes like a lunatic.

'How long were you planning on hiding back there?'

I come up alongside him, 'Proper twats,' I say. Maybe he thinks I'm a retard. Or some kind of queer, sat eye-balling him. I flick the dog-end into the water, watch it float by.

'You look like her,' he says, swatting the air. 'Bastard flies.'

He knows who I am. 'Nah,' I say. 'I look more like my old man than Birdee.'

'Me too. My old man—not yours.'

Beside him I can smell hard work and armpits. It's not bad. And when he speaks, his voice catches in the back of his throat before it leaves his mouth. I like the rough sound he makes. Recognise him from the telephone. Calling me up about Dora. And later, Fysh. Reckon he can see the realisation in the way I've come closer.

'Was me that called you.'

'Alright.' I say.

'That morning on the marsh. Saw the lights flashing two miles off.'

He means when the law came for Fysh. Doesn't matter much now, but I want to know. 'Why'd you tell me where Dora was hiding out?'

'Birdee talked about you and Tim Fysh. Way you were with one another.' He watches the lads messing about in the river. 'But he had a wife.'

152

'I know—'

'I don't mean anything by it. But she deserved to hear about him from you. After Birdee—'

'What?' I ask.

'Your old man should have been the one to tell me. Might have helped.' Shakes his head.

I don't reckon it helped me none. 'I tried.'

'Took you two years. Figured you'd turn up eventually.'

There's no blame there. Just a long row of days from Birdee to here. 'I wasn't doing good.' The Soldier is something else. He doesn't make me need to adjust my underpants. Means I can tell him the truth.

'I've seen you on the riverbank—talking to yourself,' he says.

'I'm finished with that,' I say. And mean it.

'This fucking place.' Nudges my shoulder. 'You trust me?'

I do. But I don't understand why. He kicks off his trainers. Pulls his t-shirt over his head in one practised swoop. His shoulder is fucked up like melted plastic. It's hard not to stare. Shorts heaped on the hot ground, him walking into the river. 'You coming in—or what?'

I take off my clothes and follow him into the water. Waist-deep, I ask him, 'Doesn't this make us cunts?'

'Means we're unafraid.' And he disappears beneath the surface. Comes back up, shaking his head, pieces of water as shiny as glass all over the place. 'It's just fucking water.'

Now, with our backs against the hard ground, smoking too many cigarettes, the sun dries out our soaked underpants. Eyelids closed, I'm watching colours colliding.

'You asleep?'

'Nah.'

The Soldier stretches, bones groaning like a plank of wood. 'You've something I want,' he says.

'How'd you mean?' Turn my head and open my eyes. Our noses are almost touching.

'Sell me Birdee's red boat.'

Birdee's red boat has been different colours to different people. Layers and layers of paint until nobody's left who remembers the first. I reckon memories behave in the same way. One piled upon the other until you can only see back so far.

Marooned, wrong way up, and balanced on two six-foot planks, I hunch over the keel. Pull the scraper until I'm out of reach. Working my muscles until the ache leaks out of my skin. Sweat everywhere. There's remnants of paint littering the toes of my trainers and grass beneath. Bare-chested, I work to forget. It's not easy. In this light the red paint is the same colour as Fysh's hair. Why'd he go marry Dora? Jesus, Fysh.

Nothing to be had from imagining what can't be. Birdee believes it's no bad thing. That Fysh is wrong in the same way that seeing a single magpie means trouble. She's super-stitious sometimes. Doesn't stop her from carrying on with the one-armed Soldier. I don't know anything about him. Birdee's Soldier is a riddle. Way she keeps him away from the house at the Point, and our old man. Instead, disappearing out on the marsh where his houseboat's moored in the deep grass. She reckons it's quiet out there, same as being deaf. Sometimes I wonder how he holds her. Then I'm back holding Fysh in my head, knowing there's no one else like him. Fuck.

Sun's rolled up until it can't get any higher, and I'm wiping sweaty palms across the arse of my wrecked blue cut-offs. Guzzling water from a plastic bottle that's more warm than not.

My old man's wandered here from the house. Standing like an idiot, as if he's forgotten his name. His eyes fixed on something over my left shoulder. 'What is it?' I say, capping the bottle.

'It's not good—' he says.

'Alright.'

'Your sister.'

'What about Birdee?'

'She's—dead—drowned.'

'Don't be stupid. Birdee's not dead,' I say. 'You're wrong—'

Shakes his head. 'Joe—'

If this were a film showing at the Pilot, he'd be holding me. But it's not. And he doesn't. Because he's wrong. Birdee can't be dead. He's an idiot. I'd know inside. Wouldn't I? My Birdee—I won't ever believe him.

Driving home from the lido. The Soldier, sat beside me, is staring out of the open window. River wind messing up his crazy black hair, he says, 'What do ya reckon, then?'

'Huh?' Busy watching the way ahead. Here and there lanky trees looking like big bird feathers are bored in the hot dirt.

'You'll sell me her boat?'

Might be the wind in my ears, why I'm unwilling to hear him. Yet it could be the stab in my chest imagining this place without Birdee's red boat. Seems like even now she's here meddling. Showing me the way to rid myself of Dora. Suddenly I'm not so sure I want Dora gone. And it's more than losing Birdee's boat. I like Dora.

'Alright,' I say.

'How much you want for it?'

'Dunno.'

'You changed your mind or something?'

'Nah,' I say. 'Why'd you want it so badly?'

'Be useful to have,' he says. 'And—same reason you want to hang on to it.'

I had Birdee for longer than the Soldier. 'Boat's yours. Pay me what it's worth.'

'I will.'

'There's more—'

'Go on.'

'I want to know about you and my sister.'

'Come again?'

'Stories—'

'You're an odd fucker.'

'That's what I want.'

'Deal.'

I turn off the ignition. 'You want to meet Dora?' I ask.

'Not today,' he says. 'Don't be a stranger.'

'I'll be over with Birdee's boat—soon.' Watching the shape of him walk away.

*

As the Soldier disappears into the marsh, Dora is banging on the window like a madwoman. I get out of the car. 'You scared the crap out of me.'

'That him?'

I nod.

'Bloody hell,' she says.

'He was at the lido,' I say.

'They opened it?'

'Nah. We went swimming in the river.'

'How's he manage that?'

'Alright' I say. 'We went dunking.' Weather wearing on my nerves a little bit.

'The water—you hear anything?'

'Nothing—river's stopped talking.' Birdee drowned two years ago. I know that now. My t-shirt is soaked through with sweat, and the heat is making my bollocks itch. 'I need a bath.'

'Mind the dog shit,' she says, pointing on the track.

'Fucking strays.'

'What'd you two talk about?'

'I've good news. Sold him Birdee's red boat.'

'What?'

'Means I'll have the money you need—soon.'

Dora has her hand on my arm. 'You sure? Figured you'd want to hang on to it.'

'I am,' I say. 'Besides, I want to be around him.'

'Why?'

'There's something he's not telling me about Birdee. I reckon—'

'You know what I think?' she says. 'Sunlight and blue-bottles on dog shit is a surprising kind of beautiful.'

There's all kinds of red. Ketchup, cherry, nosebleed. The red that was Fysh's hair. I'm near town, buying paint at Walker and Anderson's. The shop, tucked beside the Fenman pub, smells of turpentine and sawdust. The click-clacking is an electric fan, sat on the counter whirling dangerously out of control. The whole time I'm keeping an eye on it. Any minute it could rattle its screws loose. Injure someone. My sweaty face gets hotter waiting for the acne-spoiled lad to serve me. He's busy watching a small television, the kind that has its own aerial.

'Mate?' I say.

'So—rry,' he says.

Miserable twat. I tap the tin of paint I've chosen for Birdee's boat. Dynamite. I reckon she'd like that. If I had a stick of the stuff, I'd shove it up this lad's arsehole to hurry him up. Fuck, it's hot.

Further along the street, outside Irene's, there's boxes of fruit and veg stacked on wooden farm crates. Pears, rhubarb and lettuce take up the pavement. A nose-full of samphire, spoiling in the heat, nudges from me the feeling of rolling about on the salt marsh. I want to go inside. But there's a fat woman filling up the doorway, sucking on a filthy oxygen mask, messed up with nicotine. When she comes outside, I follow the tube trailing behind her. It goes all the way into a white metal oxygen tank, strapped to the back of a red-faced boy. I know how he feels.

I find three good peaches. It's not easy. Tear myself down a brown paper bag.

'You're a peach,' Irene says, from behind the counter. I want to be on my own. Because it's too warm to sit in the car, I put the can of paint in the boot. Walk across London Road and go to church.

God's a clever cunt, keeping the sweltering sun from coming inside. Here, in Our Lady of the Annunciation, stone's throw from where I found Dora, I'm eating a warm peach on a smooth pew. Juice leaking, messing up my chin, doing my best to keep bad language out of my head. Even though I don't care much for God, this is his house. Here there's strange stained-glass windows to watch, saints casting colour everywhere. Up front just a bare wall, Jesus Christ hanging there, minding his own business.

Until I decide to trouble him with my confession. This is the nightmare that came unstuck from my head last night. The beached whale is wrinkled like wrecked leather and stinks of hate. Fills me with dread. Even so I'm running back and forth between the shore and water, cradling palm-fuls of angry seawater. All the while the whale's big black eye following my progress. Worn knackered, I tip the last half palmful of water into its mouth. But the whale isn't a gigantic bleak beast any longer; instead Birdee's Soldier is staring up at me, his dark hair sodden. He has two good arms. Puts his hands over my ears and speaks to me. I can't hear a word, and it doesn't matter because the weight of his fingers tugging my hair feels good. Until I'm yanked awake. First thing I do is stuff my hand down the front of my underpants. I haven't pissed the bed. It's proof everything's alright. I say, 'What'd you reckon it means, Jesus?' He says nothing. Still busy hanging between here and what nobody knows.

I lick my fingers clean, let my shorts dry them off. From the brown paper bag I pull out a second peach.

'You can't eat that here.'

'Huh?'

'I think you should leave,' he says. Wearing black, his bald head has colours swimming in lazy circles. 'Right away—'

'Steady on,' I say still chewing, and go outside. Meddling bastard.

Traffics rowdy at this time, engines revving, brakes clunking, horns honking. Out the way, down the side of the church, yew trees are huddling, chucking shade onto the bench beneath. I light a Benson & Hedges, pull off my t-shirt. Lean back and let my eyelids loose.

'How's it going?'

'Fuck—' I say, startled.

'Sorry,' he says. 'Didn't mean to—'

'Alright.' He's dressed like a knob. Shirt sleeves rolled all the way up. Black jacket slung over his shoulder. His hair is canary in this light. Looks rock hard. Reckon it would take a whirlwind to shift it.

161

'Don't worry about the Father. He's a miserable twat. But harmless.'

'If you say so.'

Puts his hand out. 'Pete—'

'You work here?' I shake his hand, heavy like a house brick.

'Here, and other places. I drive dead people,' like there's nothing strange about it.

'I've seen your old man about,' I say. Fucking undertakers. Big black beetles burying dead things. Why'd anyone want to do that?

'He's not my old man,' Pete says. 'You mind?' And he takes a seat beside me. 'I work for him, that's all.'

'Alright.' Pete could be an idiot. His neatly parted hair is aching to be messed up. And there's an oddness here, leaking out of him like sweat. 'You want it?' I ask, pushing the brown paper bag along the bench till it's against his leg.

'Sure,' opening the bag and taking out the last peach. 'Cheers.'

I smoke and watch him eat. Peach all over. It worries me because I like him a little bit. First throb of a hard-on going up in my underpants. And I've folded my arms across my chest because my nipples are misbehaving all of a sudden. What if Jesus Christ can see through walls? Bet he's watching me, knowing how badly I'd like to lick the juice off Pete's chin. Instead, I flick my dog-end onto the path, get up and walk away.

'Thanks—for the peach,' he says, rubbing his palms against the legs of his black trousers.

'No worries.'

'Nice meeting you—'

'Tim Fysh,' I say, turning back. I don't know why I lied.

Round the corner from where I first found Dora, Everard Street cuts a concrete line between the launderette and Crossways pub. Outside three lads are misbehaving against the whitewashed wall. T-shirts tucked in back pockets. Necking pints. Pressed together. Their skin tan, arms muddled with ink, mixing them up. One could be the brother of the man in the purple t-shirt who promised to smash my teeth in. These lads make me thirsty.

I go inside the launderette. Boom, the heat surprising as a punch in the head. The door, wedged open, hasn't helped.

Along one wall there's a row of custard-yellow coin-operated washers. Then dryers, all the way to the back, where Dora is fanning her face with a sign that says *Out of Order.*

'Hot as hell in here,' I say.

'What's wrong?' she asks.

'Nothing. Was nearby.'

She doesn't believe me. Squeezes her eyes until it's hard to tell their colour.

'Was at Walker and Anderson's. Buying paint.' I won't tell her about the peaches and Pete, the idiot.

'Paint?'

'For Birdee's boat.'

'Right—' she says. 'He paid you yet?'

I shake my head. 'Soon.' Before long Dora will have her money and I'll not lay eyes on her again. Don't know how I feel about that.

The thump against the big glass window whips both our heads about. 'Sorry—' shouts the lad picking his trainer off the pavement.

'They'll be trouble later.'

'Reckon you're right.' Something makes me think she's more worried about the trouble standing in front of her. 'Busy?'

'Busy enough,' she says, sitting down.

I sit down beside her. The vinyl bench is hot on my backside. Fucked up with idle hands scoring hope into plastic. *Billy loves Gina*. Smells rubbish in here. Soap powder and armpits. Across from us, a single sock has my attention. Blue, and it could be hard with cum. I'm wondering where the other one has gone. What am I doing here? I came to ask her about the Soldier. See what to do about it. But now I feel stupid.

'Can hang about—if you want a lift later?'

'No. Besides, I've two hours yet.'

'Alright.' Dora does things differently. Never makes it easy. 'Been thinking—about my whale.'

'What about it?' she asks, jaw jutting forward.

I tell her my nightmare. The whale that became Birdee's Soldier. Even confessing that I hadn't pissed the bed, careful, because there's a woman further along the bench folding a stack of t-shirts. 'You reckon it means something?'

'No—I don't. Except the heat's turned you stupid.'

'Probably—' I say.

'Look—was just a nightmare—it doesn't mean anything.' Dora fiddles with her fingers. She's thinking about how a cigarette would look good right now. 'Fysh had terrible nightmares.'

Sitting beside her, heat busting all kinds of thoughts out of us, I'm suddenly sorry for Dora. Will the sight of me someday not hurt her?

'He have them with you?'

'Dunno.' Fuck.

'Said they started after he married me.'

Blame is like a cut that won't heal up. 'What was it like—' I say, 'Being married?'

'Cold,' she says. Like it's the most obvious thing ever. 'At least it was for me.'

'Fysh lied—'

'What do you mean?'

'He'd had nightmares since he was fifteen.' Would scrap around in bed like a welterweight. Never knew a thing about it come morning. 'His mum's fella beat him up. Pretty badly.'

'Never said a word.'

'Sounds like Fysh,' I get up. Pull at the back of my shorts where they've stuck to my arse. 'Alright—I'll see you later.'

'Don't worry about your dream—means nothing,' Dora says.

'You're right,' I say. 'Nothing at all.'

From here the house at the Point looks like a lighthouse beside the wet. Way the shine bounces off the upstairs window. Warning the trawlers trailing along the river what's inside. That's why we're rowing on the creek, away from our old man. An oar apiece. But the timing's all wrong. I tell Birdee that it's proper for boys to row.

'That's stupid,' she says.

Bidree's not wrong. 'Alright,' I say. 'But turn around.' Tide's full here, at the mouth of the creek. I'm worried we'll get swept into a fishing trawler on its way to the Outer Roads.

'Trust me.'

Nothing else to do but throw my head back, hunt for aeroplanes. The tracks they draw across the blue. Birdee's singing softy, and it doesn't take long before the creek gets narrow, shrinking in on us. Oars making clapping noises smacking the grassy bank.

'Was wider before,' Birdee says.

The marsh never stands still. Water has a will of its own. 'Hold on,' I say, jumping out the boat, rope in my hand. 'Widens up ahead.' I'll pull us along until the oars will work again. Suddenly I'm standing still. On my right a pool of water, so still it seems like a lump of sky has dropped onto the ground. Could be the same wet we found Mum in?

'What you looking at?' Birdee's on tiptoe in the boat, straining to see what's snagged my attention. 'That's not where she was,' she says.

'How'd you know?'

'Because—I'm smarter than you.'

'Alright,' I say, because she is. 'You want to go home?'

'No—keep going,' and Birdee starts singing, 'Row, row, row your boat—Gently down the stream—Merrily, merrily, merrily—'

I reckon, it might just be the nicest sound I've ever heard.

I'm out in the shed. Birdee's boat is Dynamite Red. I can't take my eyes off of it. 'Hope—you like it?' I ask, running my hand against the warm wood.

'Who you talking to?' Dora says.

'Nobody,' I say, feeling a little bit stupid telling Birdee things she'll never hear.

'It's really red.' Standing in the doorway, looking purposeful.

'Sure is.' Taking both sandwiches with dirty hands. 'Keep the plate.'

'How much longer—before it's finished?' Dora leans against the doorframe.

'Couple of days. Outboard needs some work.'

'Then he'll pay you?'

'Yes,' I say. 'You'll have your money.'

'Hope it'll float.'

'She'll float—' Then she's walking back to the house, and I'm wondering what bug crawled up her arse. 'Hey, Dora,' I shout. 'You alright?' But I don't think she hears me.

My back is wet with sweat. I lie down on the grass outside the shed to cool off. My fingers knitted behind my head. And I can't believe how heavy the big blue sky is, pushing down onto my face, squeezing the air out of me. Bare-chested, the breeze down here hardens off my nipples. Doesn't get much better than this.

Floodlit, the stadium trembles, a rusty cage crawling with petrolheads. The noise is crazy beside the dirt track. There's every colour thundering by. It's not easy to tell the cars apart or figure out why Dora brought me to see the bangers tonight. Yet here I am, drinking a can of beer, puzzling how she's managed to finish her second hotdog. Her lips are coloured with ketchup, eyes wide. People looking might think she's mine. That the baby inside her belly got there on a night not unlike this one. Air ruined with fuel, fucking her upright in the car park. And they'd be right in part. Because I did fuck Dora. Just not how a lad is supposed to.

Everywhere rowdy lads are bragging, bashing about, talking messed-up crap to pretty girls, while passing around shared cigarettes. This is the way things are here. If you're normal.

'Can you not read, mate? Sign says keep clear of the netting. Your bird, too.'

Dora tugs my elbow. 'Don't look for trouble where there isn't any.'

We move away, further along to a wall of worn lorry tyres, where it's quieter. I lean into the rubber, not caring if it fucks up my clean t-shirt. Light a cigarette and watch him hassling another lad. 'What are we doing here?'

'Watching the bangers,' Dora says.

'Alright—and?'

She shrugs. 'I'd kill for a cigarette.'

'Here you go.' And I try to pass her my crushed packet, worn the shape of arse from being in my back pocket. She shakes her head. I reckon it's better to give people what they ask for right away, even when you know they don't really want it after all. I make up my mind we should head home. 'Come on,' I say, pushing off the tyre wall. 'We're going—'

'Before—' she says, leaning into me. 'I went out with a speedway lad. Lost my virginity right over there.'

Glancing sideways to the place Dora's remembering, I know she's like every other girl who got ruined here. Nothing to do about it. 'Sorry,' I say.

'Don't be.'

I'm thinking about my own ghosts when she says, 'He was nothing like Fysh.'

Not hard to believe. 'Yeah?'

'You ever wonder—if things might have been different?'

'How'd you mean?'

'If we'd never known him?'

'No. I don't wonder that.' I won't consider not knowing Fysh.

She's crying a bit now. 'Who'll want me—dead husband—baby—I'm fucked.'

'You're not fucked. Don't cry.'

'Yeah—you think?'

'I want you,' I say, even if it's hard to admit out loud. 'And the baby will want you. It's everything—'

Dora looks at me like I'm finally making sense. 'You're right.'

'Happens sometimes.'

'Let's go,' she says, wiping her face on the backs of her hands.

'Nah,' I say. 'You want another hotdog?'

'God—Yes.'

'I'm buying—'

We ease back into the racket. Dora takes the empty beer can I'm still holding, drops it in the bin. Says, 'You really want me—around?'

'Huh?'

'Doesn't matter.'

I lean in. Her hair smells like fried onion and petrol, but beneath there's the marsh, salt and grass. 'I heard you,' I say. 'I'm used to having you around.'

Dora smiles. Line's not so long, and she's already licking her lips. 'What about you?'

'What about me?'

Rolling her eyes. 'Your first time—'

Don't see any point saying anything other than, 'Fysh.' Because it's the truth. 'But—there was this one girl.'

'Yeah?'

'Lillian.' Being here, how can I not think about her? 'She had the fattest crush on me.'

*

171

'I've got five minutes,' Lilian says, eyes sparkling like car lights.

She's on her break from Woody's, a mobile van that sells bad hotdogs and six-packs of warm beer. 'Alright,' I say. 'But who's watching the van?'

'My brother.'

'Fuck—really?' He'll beat the guts out of me, right here at the speedway. And nobody'll have the bollocks to stop him. 'What if he hears us?'

'What—with that racket going on?'

Lilian might be right. There's no way around this. Before I've sucked the last smoke from my cigarette, we're around back, Lillian slipping her yellow knickers over her shoes. I start kissing her, sliding my hands beneath her skirt, figuring out where to put my fingers.

She pulls away, lipstick wrecked, says, 'It's all right—you can fuck me.'

Hearing it out loud hurts. Yet I have to do this. Figuring it could help, I think on Fysh, him bucked up behind. His hands all over the place, tracing me. Though it's not working. Making me more miserable. I want to sneak away. Go anyplace else. 'Don't,' I grunt, her hand pushed down the front of my underpants. My dick does nothing. Doesn't even twitch. Just sits there against my bollocks, useless. 'Fuck.'

'You had too much to drink?' she asks.

'Nah,' I shake my head side to side. 'It's not that.'

'You queer, or something?'

'Reckon I am—'

'Fuck off.'

Some lads across the way in the carpark start whistling. They don't know I'm not fucking Lillian. Instead, she's holding me while I bawl into her tits.

Here in my room, back against the wall, watching the light abandon the marsh outside. The house is restless. These floorboards beneath my backside stretching into summer. Adjusting themselves until they're at ease. I know how they feel.

Early tomorrow morning I'll take Birdee's red boat out to the Soldier now the outboard's mended. I'm keen to see him again. Dora doesn't want to hear a word about it. As if she believes he's dangerous. Or broken, on account of him only owning the one arm. I've tried to reassure her that in every other way he's like any other man. Really, I reckon she's curious about him.

Because I'm thirsty, I go downstairs, guzzle cloudy water at the kitchen sink. In between gulps, 'Didn't mean to wake you.'

'You haven't,' Dora says, eyes rimmed red.

Lately, Dora's been bawling more often than not. Seems being pregnant is like riding the gallopers at the Mart. When you get off it feels like the world is spinning without you. Rushing by. 'What's wrong?' I ask.

'Who said anything's wrong?'

'Alright.' And I don't know much about hormones, except maybe boys behave differently. Makes me head back the way I came, preferring the warm planks on my bedroom floor.

'Don't go—' she says.

Outside it's cooler. I leave the gate swinging behind me. We're barefoot on the edge of the riverbank, following the line, out onto the marsh. Grass gliding against my shins. There's enough light left over that I don't have to worry about treading in dog shit.

We haven't gone far before Dora stops still. Where the trawler wreck used to be. If it were day there'd be a dark scar laid in the marsh. Charred wood. Spoiled ground. 'Why'd you burn it?' she asks.

'Dunno,' I say. That's not true. 'Cuz I ruined it.' When Fit Lad turned up. And I took him inside the wreck. Busted open his trousers, tugging everything down. He'd held on to the back of my head while I'd licked his balls, worked my way up until—

'Did it help?'

'Nah.' I miss stooping inside. Running my finger over our initials. Being someplace that was ours. Jesus, Fysh. 'I miss him.'

'I don't.' Loud like she's telling the river, even the tide beneath. 'Not any more.'

'Alright.' Rubbing my palms against my arms, hugging myself. It's not because I'm cold. Dora's unsettling me.

'Been thinking—about your Birdee's boat.'

'What about it?'

'Don't sell it.'

'Huh?' Why in hell would she have me keep it? Means she'd be stuck here longer. 'Don't understand—'

'Can't see how you can let it go.'

'Going in the morning, first thing,' I say. 'Figured you'd be glad.'

174

She's close to crying. 'I'm all right here—with you.'

Just like Dora to surprise the crap out of me, now night's coming in. I want to hold her. Tell her to stay. But I don't. Because I can't. Goodbye is all I know—

Everything I care about has gone away. I'm inside the wreck on the marsh, looking at our initials. 'Goodbye,' I holler. Me and Fysh. Why'd he not come? He knows about Birdee. My old man reckoned he called the house yesterday to say he was sorry. Fuck him for not telling me to my face, and I punch the wood, hard. Doesn't matter that I'm bleeding. Hands already ruined from tearing Birdee's room to pieces. I won't leave anything for the old man to remember her by. He doesn't deserve it. My Birdee. 'Goodbye,' I say. And pull myself away, out onto the marsh. The sky's not ever been bigger.

Because I'm unable to keep myself from him, my old man knows what's coming. 'I'm leaving,' I shout. 'For fucking good.'

'If that's what you want,' he says, his jaw hard.

'It's over with Fysh—'

'Good.' Folds his arms across his chest.

Hate's stubborn like that. I don't have to stomach it. All of a sudden I know invisible things are the hardest to forget. Like the time he beat me with his belt because I'm queer. That I figured out men taste of armpits and cum, are easy to get hard, and make pleasing sounds when I stir them. 'Fuck you—'

'You're a lunatic,' he says.

'Could be—'

175

'You're just like her, you know?'

My old man means my mum. He believes she was crazy. Fucked up. Ruined. And maybe she was. But I'll not stay here in this house at the Point. This fucking town. There's nothing left. Birdee disappeared. Fysh, gone and married to Dora.

Inside, I tug out the bag from beneath the bed. Stuff my t-shirts inside. A picture I care about. I don't look around like they do on television remembering rubbish. Instead, I race back outside, where he's still standing. He has a look on his face, like I'm baffling him, even now when there's nothing left he doesn't already know.

And I'm through the gate. Walking down the track, my trainers taking me away. My head aches. Bollocks, too. Spinning like a fruit machine in the Bus Cafe, I'm figuring out what to do. 'Pick one thing,' I say to myself. Don't worry about the rest. 'Go to the lido,' for Birdee. See if there's any trace of her left in the water. Something, any-thing, for me to hold on to.

Tide's hasty here, galloping along the river in Birdee's newly painted boat. Outboard's making steady noises, engine throbbing, propelling this Dynamite Red. Wouldn't come this far by paddle. Might get guzzled up by the tide, chucked onto the Outer Roads before I know what's happening.

The light right now is silvered, clinging to the last of the fog that drifted in from the open water, soon to vanish like a magic trick. Now you see it, before you didn't. My old man calls it sea smoke. When we were small he said this fog carried the dead trawler men home to their families. My old man is full of shit. I hope he never comes home.

With the river proper behind me, creek narrowing on both sides, Birdee's boat pulls itself into the marsh, returning to the Soldier. The way remembered. Barely a need to grasp the rudder. Like migrating geese, I reckon wood hangs on to memory. Has secrets buried in the grain. This marshland is ridden with the untold.

Before I've time to ready myself, the Soldier's houseboat appears. He's standing waiting for me on the wooden jetty.

'Heard you coming,' he says, scratching his chest, grinning. His feet are bare and filthy.

'Alright,' I say, outboard coming to a slow stop, leaving only marsh noises between us. I get out and tie off Birdee's red boat. There's all kinds of confusion in his eyes. He hustles me into an awkward hug.

'Good job, mate.' That voice catching in the back of his throat, telling my ear.

'You like it?'

'Like it? Hell, yeah,' he says. 'Wait here.'

I'm kicking at the dirt with the toe of my trainer, building a small mound, in two minds about Birdee and the questions I want to ask the Soldier. I thought I'd have more time to think things through.

He's back, carrying beer. Sits down nearby. 'Grab a chair.'

I go find another to put my backside against.

The Soldier grips the can between his knees, pulls the tab. Hands me the warm tin. Opens another for himself. 'To Birdee.'

'Birdee,' I say. Bet we look pretty stupid. Two of us sat on fucked-up deckchairs drinking beer, watching a red boat doing nothing special. Bobbing up, bobbing down. Flies mad about the new coat of paint.

'Here ya go.' And he hands me an envelope rammed with money.

'Looks like a lot—'

'It's a fair price.'

'Alright,' I say, stuff the money in my pocket, wondering

what Dora will say when she sees it. Her future tucked inside a grubby envelope that's already been posted. Then I take a big swig of beer, lean forward a little bit. 'I—'

'Shoot,' he says, knowing I've some things on my mind.

'Been thinking about the lido.'

'What about it?'

'Were you—'

'Fuck.' And he necks the rest of the can. Scrunches it into a messy lump, dropping it beside his feet. 'I was there. Then I wasn't.'

'Didn't mean anything by it.'

'You've seen me in the water?' he says. 'Fucking arm. Cunts staring.'

I don't say anything because there's no way around his missing arm.

'I didn't want her there, at the lido. Looking like she did. Birdee called me an idiot. But I fucked off anyway with a mate.'

'Alright.'

'But it wasn't. I was being a jealous twat. Figured I'd go back and tell her. But she was pretty messed up.'

'How'd you mean?'

'She'd been drinking with that ginger cunt.'

'Huh?'

'Your Fysh's brother—what's his name?'

'Doug,' I say, sound of his name agitating me.

'Yeah, Doug. Handsome twat. Him and Birdee were fighting about something. You know Birdee—she was doing most of the fighting. Told him I'd fuck him up if he didn't get lost.'

'What'd he do?'

'Nothing much. Told Birdee to stay away was all.'

'How come?'

'Fuck.' Look in his black eyes says he's unsure to tell me. 'Birdee said they were arguing about you. He warned her to keep you away from Fysh—with him being newly married.'

For ages I don't know what to say. My head all over the place.

'You all right?'

I want to tell him that nothing is right. 'Why'd you leave her there?'

The Soldier looks sorry and furious together. Like he's asked himself a thousand times already. 'She wouldn't come home,' he says. 'I tried—but she was drinking.' Then he closes his eyes, seeing something I never will. 'Last time I saw her—'

Getting up, I say, 'Have someplace to be.'

'I shouldn't have left her alone—it's my fault, I know.'

'Nah.' Birdee never needed looking after. 'What about Doug?'

'What about him?'

'He there when you left?'

'What's it matter?'

'Guess it doesn't.' And I walk away.

'You want me to take you home in the boat?'

'You won't make it back before the tide.'

'Right—'

Running like a bastard through the marsh towards the house at the Point. Because it's not the beer or the heat-boiling

sweat that's agitating me. But Doug warning me off Fysh.
He had no business with Birdee. Fysh had already taken
care of it on the quay beneath the brick shelter. Pleading for
his chance with Dora. Wanting me to give over. Not make
it any harder on him. Fysh could conjure the tide to turn if
he wanted. And I'm wondering, maybe Doug could too—

I'm stirred up. Dora's not hearing me. What I'm telling
her means something big. Instead, she's fiddling with a jam
jar rammed with purple flowers on the windowsill. Stupid
flies, shiny with summer, are buzzing about, unable to find
the sky through the gap at the bottom. Outside the river's
rolled back, sun baking tide mud. Smells like warm clay in
the kitchen.

'Birdee and Doug could've been fighting about anything,' she says. 'Leave it alone.'

'Nah,' I say. 'Soldier said Doug was warning Birdee to
keep me away from Fysh.'

'That must be it, then.'

'Doesn't make sense.' I'm mad Dora's uninterested.
She's been behaving badly since I busted back through the
kitchen door. 'Cuz I'd told Fysh already that I'd stay away.'
There's the riddle. 'Did Fysh say anything to you?'

'About what?'

'Doug going on at Birdee.'

'He didn't.'

The whole while Dora's been stood at the kitchen sink,
her back to me. I'm leaning against the wall, something
else bothering me. The envelope is sat on the table, where
I'd put it before. Untouched. She's not wanted me to sell

Birdee's boat all along. Why not, I'm wondering? 'You not gonna count the money?'

'Later.'

'Alright.' Unfolding my arms from across my chest. 'I'm going out—'

'Where to?' Dora asks. 'You've just got in.'

'See Doug. Find out what the hell's going on.'

'Forget about it.'

'No,' I yelp.

Now there's purple all over the sink. Glass glistening. 'Jesus Christ— Please—'

'I won't.' Coming across the kitchen floor. 'I can't.' Gathering Dora's scattered flowers. Bits of broken jar.

'Leave it.' Dora pulls out a chair, puts herself in it, tells me to do the same.

My bollocks haven't ached for some time. Thought maybe they'd forgotten how. I am mistaken. Lighting a cigarette gives me something to do. 'What's wrong?' She won't look at me.

'I knew right away I'd made a terrible mistake,' she says, rolling a piece of loose skin torn from her bottom lip between her thumb and forefinger.

'How'd you mean?' I ask. What's this got to do with Birdee? And the ache is a signpost. Big and bright. Telling me that whatever comes next I won't want to hear. I'd cover my ears if it'd do any good.

'I thought Fysh'd be different. After we married. That he'd changed. But he still had an itch that needed scratching—you.'

That's not my doing. 'I left him be. Like he wanted.'

Dora shakes her head. 'Then your Birdee drowned, and you went away. It was better for a while.'

'Wasn't for me.'

'I know that.'

'Do you?'

'Yes.'

'Glad you and Fysh were better without me.'

'Not Fysh. He got worse. Nightmares too. He'd disappear for days. Out on the water.'

'He never told me.' Any of it. 'That why you left him?'

'He stopped—wouldn't touch me.'

Dora's not making sense. What about the baby?

'I wanted to hurt Fysh. For what he did to me.'

'What'd he do?'

She's looking at me like I'm an idiot. Like it's the most obvious thing in the world. 'He wanted you—more than me.' Now she's crying. No noise. Just a trail of tears. 'Fysh isn't the father.' She says it fast, like ripping off a plaster.

'Huh?' Because that can't be true. Dora's here because of the baby. For Fysh. The chance I'd promised him in my head. 'Who, then?' But I already know. Doug. 'How fucking could you?'

'I didn't mean—'

'Dunno how I didn't see.' All of it. She's right. I'm an idiot. Doug knows. My old man might too. Nothing would surprise me. I get up. But I don't know where to go. Reckon if I stay standing here I'll do something stupid. 'Take the money. Go.'

'I tried to tell you,' Dora says. 'But then everything—'

'What?' Small voice, like I'm starting over.

'Seemed better. Like it would be all right.'

Nothing's right. Not even a little bit. Been shaking my head since she began. I'm confused. And thirsty. I reckon my head's turning inside out. What's on the outside doing its best to get away. 'Where's Birdee fit in?' This riddle running through me; Doug on the riverbank talking rubbish. Saying, Shame it was Birdee and not me.

'Doug,' Dora says, though she doesn't look at me. 'Did the same to Birdee.'

'Same what?' I ask.

'He got her pregnant.'

'Nah—can't be.' Dora is a lying cunt.

'That's what they fought about at the lido—Doug warned me—he'd do the same to me—if I told anyone.'

'Same?'

'Kill—me—' Dora says.

'Huh?' My balls hurt badly. Even holding on to them doesn't help any. Teeth gritted. I'm afraid. There's trouble here, only blackness.

'He drowned her.'

Some things will never be alright to hear.

After dark, and the lido is still. Palm hugging concrete. Fingertips red raw from ripping paper from the walls of her room. Forgetting about my old man and everything that he is. I'm lying on the cool ground, other arm steadying myself, easing my ear into the water. Listening for sister sounds beneath the wet. I am afraid to go into the inky water. This place is a thief. Takes what it wants.

'Mate,' he says. 'You fucked up, or what?'

He shouldn't be here either. Rolling onto my back, I tell him I'm alright. 'Seeing how cold the water is—that's all.'

'And?'

'It's alright.'

'You wanna go swimming?' And already he's cracking open his trousers, a ladder of dark hair. 'Fucking roasting.'

'Nah,' I say, getting up. 'Not tonight.'

He grins like he knows more about me than I know about myself. Maybe he does. But it doesn't matter, because I'm leaving here tonight. This town.

'I'm off—'

'Where you going?'

'Dunno,' I say. Because I don't.

'You want a lift?'

'Alright.' He'll take me someplace else. Lose me.

Outside, his car is parked beneath a streetlamp. The colour has soaked into the pavement beneath the tyres. I slide in beside him. Stinks like an old bed.

'Name's Jimmy,' he says.

There's a tattoo of the Virgin Mary on his neck. I lean across and lick the ink. Tastes like trouble.

'That's more like it—' And he guns the engine, stealing away.

Dora's eyes are burned red. It hurts too much to look at her. I wasn't sure I'd be able to walk out of here. But my legs are doing fine. The fucking heat. The goddamn buzzing. Outside on the riverbank, the water is black and calm. Looking back at me.

I want to be with Fysh. Maybe he'll be beneath the

surface. Waiting for me. Red hair the road to him. Tug my t-shirt over my head. Kick off my trainers. Shorts and underpants. Mudflats warm beneath the soles of my feet. Shouting, someplace behind me. Fuck her. Fuck all of them. He's waiting for me. Currents quickening, tugging at the tops of my legs. Cold water dissolving the ache in my bollocks. Tingling, like Fysh is down there busy with his tongue. Fingers finding the surface, feeling the swell. Moving up. Moving down. Tipping myself in half and plunging my head into the wet. Screaming his name—until the water chases the sound back down my throat into my belly. Up and guzzling air. Saying to myself—Row, row, row your boat—gently down the stream— I'm beneath the surface, turning. Rolled in rows and rows of folded black. Taken by the river—merrily, merrily, merrily, merrily—Flashes of hot. Streaks of red—life is but a dream.

If this is death, I will be alright. Not so terrible. Beneath bruised darkness, light is forgotten here. There's no river washing over my aching skin. No tide taking me wherever it pleases. Rough palms on my chest and stomach tell that the wet hasn't yet followed me to the after-place. But the smell of mud and sweat gnaw at my nostrils. Is this relief I feel? I don't reckon it can be, because I'm bawling, tears pooling at my earlobes. Fysh, where are you? And it's not his sound I'm hearing, telling me tender things I ache to hear. Instead, the rubbish he tells me. 'You're safe,' he says. 'I've got you.' The Soldier. He stole me from the river. Yanked me back from the in-between. But what about Fysh? It's not how it's meant to turn out. I fucking hate all his guts. Wrapped in this dirty fucked-up blanket. Fysh, I'm sorry—

The Soldier says I've been asleep for two days. He's at the foot of what I reckon must be his bed. Watching. Leaves me to suppose I'm on his houseboat, out on the marsh. Away from the house at the Point, and Dora. Fucking liar that she is. Everything rushing into my head at once. His stare hounding me until relief comes with watching the wall. The paint is rippled like wet sand, fingers tracing the tideline. After a time I say, 'You pulled me out the river?'

'Yes,' he says. 'Wasn't easy. Hauled you to the bank. Thought Dora would give birth there in the mud. Was an effort getting you into the boat.' Then he's silent, an unfamiliar look about his eyes, reminding me how little I know about him. 'Foolish thing to go and do.'

'Was it?' Why'd you just not let me drown?

'Don't be stupid. Besides—river didn't want you. Tide turned you over to me.'

He's talking rubbish. I want to get up, go outside, but don't know where my clothes are. I roll over. 'My clothes?'

'Table.'

I get out of bed. My legs are unsteady. Yet I won't let him help me. I feel like an idiot, stark bollock naked. Balancing myself, arms as useless as oars out of water. Across from where I'm standing is a small pine table. Behind that, a white sink. Above the tap a window hangs open. But there's no breeze, like the air's not welcome here.

The ache easing, I try for the table. 'How'd you get these?' There's pairs of everything. Two t-shirts. Two underpants. Two pairs of shorts. Like the fucking ark. 'My trainers?' I don't see any.

'You'll get 'em—when I can trust you.'

'What?'

'Don't want you doing a runner.'

'Can run barefoot,' I say, pulling up my shorts, leaving the cord lose.

'But you'll be easier to catch.'

Fuck. 'Where's my fucking trainers?' I yelp. But I'm drowning in here and can't wait any longer. I shoot outside, suck in the marsh air. Until I'm full up.

'You okay?'

'What's it look like?'

'Don't be a fucking smart-arse.'

Birdee's red boat is bound to the wooden dock, rope taut as a circus tightrope. I track alongside and piss into the muddy water. Over my shoulder I ask, 'How'd you get my things?'

'Dora.'

She's a fucking liar. Tricking Fysh into believing her belly was full up with his baby. Makes me wonder if she'd have carried around that secret for a lifetime. It boils my piss. 'I'm leaving—' but the Soldier won't let me by. He's taller than I am. Wider, too. Though I've both arms.

'No—you'll stay here. For now.' And he lights a cigarette, passes it to me. Then another for himself. Watching for trouble. 'Dora'll do fine on her own. Your old man's getting out of hospital end of the week.'

Like I care. They fucking deserve each other. 'Don't see how you'll keep me here.'

'Won't be easy,' he says. 'But you'll wish I hadn't tried when I'm done with you.'

'Nah. If you fucking knew—' And now I can't say it out loud. I'm afraid to tell him the truth. Because I don't reckon it will set him free. Thing is, in my experience, truth is like the river. Runs both ways, back and forth. And there's really no telling what's beneath the surface. Could be just an empty swell all the way down to the bottom. Or a gigantic fucking whale, with a big black boulder eyeballing you. 'Birdee didn't—'

'Settle down—' Closing the gap between us, until I can feel his breath on my chin. 'I know what you can't tell me. I talked to Dora.'

'What'd she tell you?' More lies.

'Everything—' he says. The smoke from his cigarette whirling around his head, making him look like somebody else. Then a moment later, himself once more. 'She's afraid of Doug. Believes he'd have killed her too, rather than the truth come out. Said it's why she left like she did.'

Dora has a way with words. I'm wondering if she's tricked him. Like she did my old man. And Fysh. Made them believe the blame belonged elsewhere. I don't know about that. All I want is Doug dead for what he did to my Birdee. Don't see for a single second why the Soldier doesn't feel the same. 'What about Birdee?'

'Doug pays for what he's done.'

'How?' I want to know. 'What, we tell the law?'

'Something like that.'

'Why are we standing here—talking about it?'

'Because I say so.'

Fuck him. 'Bollocks—we have to—do something.'

'You need to listen—or I'll beat the shit out you.'

'But Doug—'

The Soldier takes a solid step forward. He means it. 'Had near two fucking days to think on it. You have to trust me.'

Why should I trust him? He left Birdee by herself at the lido. If I were him, Doug would be dead already. 'Do I?'

'Birdee trusted me. Asking you to do the same.'

Everything's agitating me. This situation. All the things I wish I didn't know. Yet I won't fucking bawl in front of him again. I put my back to him. Pace about a bit. Take big eager drags on my cigarette before flicking the dog-end into the creek. Watch the tide take it away. Maybe I'm jealous. Eventually, that smoked cigarette will be swept out to the Outer Roads. Away from here. This place where misery grows taller than the grass.

'Joe,' he says, his hand on my shoulder turning me around.

Now I'm against his chest. He's hugging me tightly. While I cry. Big heaving sobs that frighten the crap out of me, worried that I'll never be able to stop again.

When I'm finished bawling, the Soldier says, 'Come on. Get back inside.' Dares me not to.

I can't run home. I am defeated. 'Alright,' I say. Beneath this small promise to the Soldier is Fysh messing about in his green underpants. Teasing with his hard-on. I can hear him, clear as glass. Telling me I'm wrong to believe there's things he wants that'll never be alright. Fysh didn't care about rules. Instead, he made it up as he went along, grinding away at the rough edges until they wouldn't draw blood. But what about me? I know what I want. To hold his brother beneath the wet until his eyes turn upside down, colouring the river red.

191

I am apprehended. But this is not a prison. I'm watched. Yet he leaves me alone. Living stacked up together, we ebb and flow like tidewater. There's a rhythm here. The Soldier could tap out the beat. We've no more control over it than the oystercatcher piping. This is what it means to surrender to the marsh. Days are light. The nights more than black, and gigantic. With nowhere to hide, I am exposed. When I need to take a shit, the Soldier goes outside, smokes a cigarette, while I sit on a portable toilet behind a mucky brown curtain at the rear of the houseboat. There's no electricity. Just a beaten-up generator I kick two times a day. Sometimes three, when it's fooling around. And when cooking can't beat back the stink of our armpits, we wash together. Taking turns under a trickle of cold water. He's rigged a shower outside, where we stand bare-arsed on the marsh, talking about important things like fried or scrambled eggs. He reckons if we wash separately, we'd run the tank dry by summer's end, before the rain can fill it up.

His mate, Cooper, comes by every few days.

Miserable-looking twat with a shaved head, and narrow eyes I've not once seen the colour of. Fills up the generator. Drops off carrier bags stuffed with food and packs of cigarettes. They talk in short bursts, like gunfire. He looks a little bit familiar. When I ask the Soldier about him, he tells me I know his brother.

'Nah,' I say. 'Don't reckon I do.'

'Lives on London Road,' he says.

'The twat in the purple t-shirt.'

'Huh?'

'Never mind—'

'He's Dora's ex-boyfriend. Bit fucked in the head. Speedway smash.'

'Makes sense.' Didn't know for sure he had a thing with Dora. Suddenly I'm thinking about the night watching bangers, stuffing hotdogs together.

'Heard he wasn't too happy she left like she did.'

I didn't fucking ask her to show up on the riverbank. 'Nothing to do with me. How'd you know his brother?'

'Served together.'

'Alright.'

'He's helping me out—while I'm minding you.'

'That what this is, then. You afraid I'll get back in the river?'

'No.' His eyes say something else. Might be kindness.

I'm keen on him, too. Still, I tell him, 'Can look after myself.'

'I've seen.'

'I could just go.' He's given me my trainers already. Got tired of looking at my dirty feet.

'But you won't,' he says. And he's not wrong. I'm not hell-bent on taking off until he's come clean with what he means to do about Doug. 'When you're ready—we'll talk about what's on your mind.'

'How'd you know I'm not ready now?'

'My nuts say otherwise.' And he pulls me into his good side, before pushing me off towards the houseboat and the meal that needs cooking. 'Get inside before we get bitten to fuck.'

And since I've been believing in the wisdom of my own bollocks for some time now, I agree. 'Alright.'

Sun splashing down on us. We're in Birdee's red boat on the tidal creek. Water's glass-clear to the bottom, feels like levitating. There's inky eels looping around and shiny fish darting. Every now and again the Soldier cracks open his eyes. 'You good?' he asks. Flies buzzing about his head.

'I'm alright,' I say. Mostly I mean it.

'Keep an eye on the tide. Don't wanna get stuck out here.'

'Wouldn't bother me.' Being misplaced here, in nobody's land. Unruly. The tide comes and goes like one huge breath. And all this happens in between the rise and fall. Like a big trick.

'You thinking about Birdee and Fysh?'

'Nah,' I say. Then suddenly I am a little bit.

'That's good.'

I drop backwards into the wet. Making a splash. And sink beneath, cold water folding into me—thinking about how near they feel. When my lungs burn to busting, I rise. 'Better,' I splutter.

'Twat,' he says. 'Stop fucking about.'

Windows are black rectangles to nothing. Door propped open to give the heat a chance to get out. The Soldier's hunched at the kitchen table, reading. He's practised at turning the pages. Makes pleasing swooshing sounds, like those I reckon you'd hear in the desert at night. A caravan on the dunes. Dry noises, nothing like the river running. I'm stretched out on the bed, just looking at moths smashing their wings against the light bulb. At this hour, I could stay here for good. Soothed by the generator, I reckon being around him is not like knowing other men. He's no interest in flipping me over to get at my arsehole. The Soldier is different. Like the brother I didn't get, and something more. But I can't quite see what.

'Mind if we call it a night?' he says, closing his book, and stretching in the awkward way he does, palm pressed against the ceiling. 'Better.'

'Alright,' I agree.

He sits down on the bed beside me, while I move over to make more room for him. But he stops me, taking hold of my jaw, tipping my head into the yellowed light, where he can get a better look at the mark on my face. 'Been thinking about this—after everything you've told me.'

'What about it?'

'Shaped like a whale,' he says, running his thumb against my temple. It scratches.

'Was born with it,' I say. Used to be nothing much more

than a stain. But it's turning darker, looking like a tattoo. Fysh said he could taste the sea when he licked me there. 'You reckon it means something?' Seems like maybe I was marked to be followed. Whale's been chasing my heels all along. 'Like a curse or something—'

'Doesn't mean nothing.'

I don't believe the Soldier. I reckon we're all marked in some way or another. Fysh with his red hair, going off early like a firework. Me and my whale tattoo. Something never means nothing. 'Why'd you bring it up, then?'

'Just thinking—about the way things are,' he says, scratching his scruffy black beard.

'How'd you mean?'

'Way we put meaning on the things that happen to us.'

'Dunno what you're getting at.'

'We make shit up—to make sense of it.'

'That in the book you're reading?' I say, nudging him.

'Put the fucking light out.'

Chucked into blackness, I don't want to sleep. Chewing on the imagined shit. The river. Birdee. Wondering about what would've happened if I'd never come back here. If that day on the shore, when a giant stretched out before me, stinking of death, I'd have just went into the sea. Would Fysh be gone still?

S torm-watching under a sticky sky, my shorts rotten with sweat, Soldier says, 'Skin's like fly paper.'

'Sweltering,' I say, wishing for rain. We're flopped on the bank, dunking our feet in the cool creek. Lightning spilling here and there, making the hairs on my arms pay attention. 'Reckon we should head inside.' Give in to the weather.

'You afraid or something?'

'Nah.' Another spark slicing up the sky. 'I'm not—'

'You wanna help me out with something?'

'Huh?'

'Come on,' he says, and I follow him to the houseboat.

Inside, he's lit the gas, boiling up a kettle's worth of water. 'What'd you reckon—' he asks. 'You up for it?'

'Alright.' His beard is unruly, like a pirate's. Must be itchy as hell in this heat.

'You'll need scissors first.' He sits down on the kitchen table, facing the open window, where the light can get at him.

It's not easy, chopping off a beard. Scissors sawing more than cutting. Metal yawning. Fuck.

'You ever do this with Fysh?'

'Not really.' Half a truth, and his eyes don't buy it. 'One time—but I didn't finish.' When Fysh was bored, his hands got busy.

'Right—' the Soldier says. 'Sounds easy to be with.'

'He was,' I say, filling up the kitchen sink. The Soldier leans over, gathering wet like a ladle, splashing his face with hot water. I squirt a wad of white foam from the can into my palm, start rubbing up his beard. I've made a proper mess with the scissors. I use my plastic razor to shave him, because it was new when he gave it to me and has plenty of bite left. But I'm still thinking on Fysh. Easy. Wasn't always like that. But we made a deal after he first fucked me in the trawler wreck on the marsh. Some agreements get made with a handshake. Others by banging shoulders until we were unafraid to touch. Untroubled with our hard-ons. That's how it was with Fysh and me.

Now the Soldier's skin's shining through where it didn't before. 'What about Birdee?' I say. 'You miss her?'

'Terribly,' he says.

I feel stupid for asking, and rinse the razor in milky water, tapping against the aluminium. Get busy scraping his neck. 'Storm's closer.' Thunder clapping.

'Birdee loved this weather—wild like it is.'

He's telling the truth. 'Mum did, too.'

'Birdee talked about her a lot.'

'She did?' I'm wondering what secrets she spilled here in this place with him.

The Soldier nods his head. There's a darkness in his eyes that wasn't there before. 'Said your mum was troubled— worried she'd wind up the same.'

Birdee reckoned it was inescapable, snapping at her heels like the river. I didn't believe her. And now they're both dead. 'Reckon I might be—just like them.'

'Doubt it.'

'How'd you know?' Maybe he's seen what troubled them in the soldiers he served with?

'Just cos. You about finished?'

'Almost.'

'You hear that?'

'Yep.'

'Come on—' and we're outside, wriggling free from our shorts. Bare-arsed and laughing like lunatics. Thunderstorm hammering hair against our foreheads. And I'm looking at the Soldier lit by lightning.

'What?' he asks.

'You look like somebody else.' His beard all over the floor inside.

'Handsome as fuck, you mean?'

'Not terrible,' I tell him.

'Twat.' he says. 'You know, you really do look like her.'

'Sorry,' I say. But I'm not.

The Soldier moves me from the edge of sleep. Roused with familiar noises. Tin kettle wailing. Chair legs raking across wooden floorboards. His lighter sparking. Hot flint. I get out of bed. Mutter, 'Morning,' on the way outside to use the tidal creek.

Like the day before, I stand, alternating between slurps of piping tea and greedy drags on my cigarette. Watching the marsh wake up. Reckon I can just about hear grass growing. From here I can see the purple river turned upside down in the sky. I know that somewhere over there Dora is making breakfast for my old man.

'You're quiet,' he says, coming alongside me.

'I'm alright.'

'Out with it.'

'Thinking about Dora. My old man. They deserve each other.'

'Don't hate Dora.'

'Why not? She's a lying cunt.'

'Steady on,' he says. 'Don't think it's that easy.'

'Dora fucked Doug.'

'Seems like she had her reasons.'

'You defending her?'

'No. But you were sucking her husband's dick.'

All of a sudden my face feels on fire. Even if I could forgive Dora, 'What about Birdee? Dora knew—the whole time.' I'm done talking about this. I'll not wait any longer. 'Doug won't walk away from this.'

The Soldier puts his hand on my shoulder, kneading the knot, a pebble of hate beneath the surface. 'Doug'll get what's coming to him,' he says. 'Promise you that—'

The whale is coming after the *Ann Marie*. Don't ask me how I know. It's not because the water is dangerously still, glass-like. And I don't have second sight like the Amazing Esmeralda, who could peer beneath the surface, all the way to the bottom, without getting wet. The gigantic beast hasn't once busted through the calm to guzzle a greedy breath. And yet it's stalking us. I can feel it in my balls. The ache. My whale has our scent, the stench of the fishing trawler. Whales can smell death 5,000 miles away, or more, I reckon.

This situation is serious. And I'm feeling like rubbish. Doug's wrists are tied tight, bound with shiny blue nylon rope. He's whining about his throbbing tailbone, banged up when the Soldier's mate kicked his legs from beneath him. His underpants are translucent with sweat. Body bruised and pale in the early light. His chest could be ruined with blood. Hard to tell from where I'm standing. Or it might be his red hair. Nipples like bullet holes.

Cooper, the Soldier's mate, is steering us towards the

Outer Roads. His brother, eyes hooded, sits watching Doug like a black guard dog. The Soldier's by my side, talking into my ear. Doesn't matter what he says, I understand nothing will be the same.

'Easy—' he tells me, his lips pressed against my earlobe. 'This is what you've been waiting for.'

There's no use denying it. Looks different here on the water, though, being pursued by the creature I believed had left me alone. When I lick my lips I can taste tar soap where I haven't rinsed my face properly. We left the houseboat fast when Cooper and Stu showed up, pounding on the door. I spit onto the deck. 'How long you been planning this?'

'Since I pulled you from the river—'

Lied to me from the start. 'Why'd you not tell me—before?'

'You weren't ready.'

'Now I am?'

'Yes.'

What's ready mean, anyway? Set for what? There's all kinds of questions whirling around my head. 'How'd you get him on the *Ann Marie*?'

'Wasn't hard. He's a fucking drunk. Easy to take.' Shifting his gaze to Cooper and his brother.

This is real. Now I know that all along the Soldier did want something from me. I screw my eyes shut. Fysh is there, watching. His stare bright with all kinds of trouble. 'This isn't happening.' It's fucked up. Even the wind's blowing the wrong way.

'It's happening all right. You had better believe it. Come on—' His hand massaging my neck. 'Don't tell me this isn't what you want—for Birdee.' Stops kneading me and lights a cigarette.

'What gives?' Stu asks.

'Nothing you need worry about,' the Soldier says, eye-balling him.

Dora's ex fucking hates me. He's a loose cannon. I watch him tug down the front of his shorts, take hold of his dick and start pissing all over Doug, who flaps about on the deck like a landed fish. It's about the saddest thing I've ever seen. His brother breaks up the situation, shouting from the wheel to, 'Settle the fuck down.'

Doug lies still, eyes wide open, watching nothing. I reckon he's found his in-between place. Who's there waiting for him?

'Don't pity him,' the Soldier says. 'You forget what he did to Birdee?'

I remember.

'Hey,' I say, digging into Doug with my right trainer. Spare eye on the Soldier huddled with the other two.

He busts up from the deck as if I've stung him, puts his back against the railings. 'What now?' Doug asks.

I sit down on a hunk of metal I've no idea the use of. It's rough with rust, and warm as a rock lying in the hot. For a time I watch him. He doesn't know I'm stilling myself inside. Swallowing the hate I'm afraid might seep through my surface. My nostrils are ruined with the stink of him. 'Why'd you do it—drown Birdee?' Nothing to lose here.

Doug looks at me like I'm an apparition. 'You killed my brother.'

205

I say, 'This isn't about Fysh.'

Baiting me. 'Yeah—it is.'

He'll never lay the blame down someplace else. I know that.

'You're exactly like her. Gone in the head.'

Gone—in—the—head. Birdee might have been unwound. But she wasn't somewhere else when she was here. 'You're wrong—shut the fuck up.'

'You ruin people.'

I want to drag him into the wet. Let the whale take him. But I don't. Instead, I get up. Done with this.

'I didn't kill Birdee—' he says, suddenly eager to talk.

Still a lying cunt. 'You'd say anything—'

'She did it all by herself.'

I can't hear this.

'She was fucked up. That bitch messed up everyone she came near.'

'Nah—' And I'm shaking my head.

'Me and Birdee were fucking around long before that one-armed cunt. She's never not been chasing after me.'

'You're a liar.'

'Fuck, I'm amazed she lasted long as she did.'

Are me and Birdee even two people? I wonder right about now. How's it come about that this red-headed cunt has more of her than me. How'd he hypnotise her? Trick her into trailing around after him, wanting something he'd never give her?

'Figure we're tit-for-tat,' Doug says.

'Huh?' I want to beat these stories to nothing. Lose them over the side. But I can't move.

'I want my fucking brother back—'

And now the Soldier has hold of Doug's hair, promising him, 'Time for talking's done.'

I put my back to the situation. I've everything to lose.

Hate gets everywhere. Can see it plain as day now the sun's chucked shadow all over the place. Doug is telling the Soldier he's wrong. Saying all kinds of rubbish to get himself off the mudflats and back on board the fishing trawler. Dodging his fate by any means. The Soldier's cut the rope binding his wrists. Doug can't run. There's nowhere to go out here. They're standing in a foot of dirty water. He's lobster red along one side. Burned by hours sprawled on deck, waiting for the tide to turn. We've come past the Outer Roads, further to where the fishing grounds are ruined. Abandoned. The brothers are smoking, watching from the railing, like crows perched on a rusty fence.

The Soldier punches Doug hard in the head. 'Why—' he howls.

Doug stands hunched and hopeless, his head going from side to side. 'I never touched her.'

'You killed her.'

'No—' And now he's grinning like a lunatic.

'Saw you arguing with her that day at the lido.'

'Was fucking her—that much is true. She reckoned she was pregnant. Baby was mine. But could just as easily been—'

Doug buckles into the wet, the Soldier's gut punch keeping him on his knees, dirty water whirling all around him. He's looking back over his shoulder, like the

Soldier's not really there. Maybe he knows my whale's coming, too.

'Fucking liar.'

'She killed herself. Just like her fucking mother. Crazy bitches.'

'No,' the soldier growls, 'Birdee'd never—'

The Soldier has his head in his hands, like suddenly the weight is too much for his neck. He's muttering to himself. But I can't hear what. Tide's coming in faster. Because I don't have any choice about it, I climb down the ladder, into the water, move over to the Soldier and Doug.

Doug says, 'Dora—was a mistake.'

'Huh?' The Soldier grunts.

I know where he's going with this.

'Didn't mean for it to happen.' Doug stands up. 'She came to me about Fysh. Next thing I know, she's fucking pregnant.'

'You fucking cunt—'

And I'm holding back the Soldier, 'Wait,' I say. 'Wanna hear this.'

'Dora threatened to tell Fysh.' Now Doug is bawling a little bit. 'Couldn't have that,' he says. 'Fuck—told her I'd killed Birdee. To get rid of her. But it was a lie. A stupid fucking lie.'

'You piece of shit,' the Soldier says. 'You're gonna fucking die out here.'

There's snot and blood all over Doug's face. Like camouflage. But beneath, he's just Doug. A fucking cunt. A brother. Jesus, Fysh. Will I ever be free of you?

*

If Fysh were here now, I'd tell him what a whale of a mess he's made of everything. Get coloured like Birdee's boat, and a little bit big-mouthed. He'd stand by, stubbornly waiting for the trouble in me to ebb away. Because he already knows some things I don't. By now his eyes'd be shiny, hypnotising, conjuring something I've never had a name for. And I'd forget about the rest. Watch it disappear. All the wrong ruining us. We'd tug our t-shirts over our heads, get lost in the shape of each other. Tracing the pretty patches of light on his chest.

Light looking as something more than brightness.

Birdee killed herself. Like my mum before her. I might never know why. But I'll not stand in this water rushing everywhere and watch Doug die for something he didn't do. The Soldier will understand. I turn myself towards him, my face close enough to feel his breath. 'He's telling the truth—we should let him go.'

'You fucking poofter,' the Soldier snarls.

If he had hit me in the face it would have hurt less.

'No fucking way you're chickening out on me now.'

'Not about that,' I say, trying to hide the sting.

'What then?'

'Birdee killed herself.' Maybe right now I look enough like her that he'll hear me.

'No—he deserves this.'

'Reckon enough people died already.'

'Get the fuck back on the boat. If you can't stomach it.'

I want to. I reckon my whale's in deeper water, close by, waiting for the Soldier to make up his mind about Doug. 'Can't do that,' I say.

'Fuck,' he hollers, sending gulls skyward. 'I figured you were ready for this. Was I wrong?'

And it comes to me that I don't know anything big about him. How he lost his arm. Nothing that counts. The stories he promised me, untold. Instead, I know what eggs he eats. The awkward shape of him when he stands beside the creek. The noise he makes reading. How he smells in half-light. Even now, I can't figure out where he keeps all the hate hidden. 'You know he didn't kill Birdee,' I say. 'Reckon you always have. You hate him—because Birdee cared about him. Maybe more than you. He's ruined her for you.'

The Soldier puts his back to me. And I watch him leave us in the tide, struggle up the ladder, onto the *Ann Marie*. Still beside me, Doug's breath is noisy, big, ragged gulps going up and down with the swell. 'This wasn't for you,' I tell him. But for Birdee. And Fysh. And my whale, who doesn't want me now.

Engine roaring like a lion. We're all on board the *Ann Marie*. Cooper on the wheel, and Stu watching me like I'm a big cunt for saving Doug's skin. Fuck them both. Doug is huddled against the railing, holding on hard in case someone decides to throw him over. I gave him back his clothes. Not uttered a word to anyone. Maybe he never will.

The Soldier won't look at me. He's standing still, horizon ahead of us. But I say it anyway. 'You did the right thing.'

He shakes his head slowly, like it hurts. 'I figured if anyone'd understand—it'd be you.'

'What good'd come from it? More fucking death?' And we stand here like this until the open water turns to river.

The water here is chasing the mud up the riverbank, unsettled in the wake of the *Ann Marie*. The house at the Point is on our left side. Looking lazy in the afternoon light. Soldier says, 'You should go home—Joe.'

Don't know where hate goes when you let it leave. I see now where the Soldier hid his hate. Inside of me. But I don't want it. 'I'm not him any more,' I say. 'All the Joe in here is gone.'

From my pocket I take out what I've come here about: two lads smiling. A picture of Fysh. Only one I have. It's folded in two. The crease shiny and smooth with wear. On the other half is Doug. They've stupid grins. No way to know what put them there. Don't remember why I haven't ripped it in two before now. Stole it in the first place, long time ago.

My old man laid out the news. Read it in the local paper. Sat across from me at the kitchen table. The Soldier got in a fight in the Greenland. Killed Doug Fysh with a broken bottle. Wild like an animal. First thought was to drive into town. See if they'd let me see him. But my old man said they'd have moved him on by now. Called him a murderer. A one-armed madman. Wanted to know if I knew why he did it. I told him I didn't. Probably over a woman, he decided.

Still wondering what these brothers are smiling about when he says, 'Hey—you looking for someone?'

'Yeah,' I say. 'You—'

Look on Pete's face is everything all at once. I'm a little bit glad he's pleased to see me. Though it could be better not to care.

'Won't be long.'

And I lean against the painted brick wall in the yard of Carter and Sons. Smoke my cigarette while watching him hose off a hearse. His shirtsleeves rolled to his elbows, the spray making pretty patterns in the dry air. This photograph in my pocket feels like it's burning a hole in my underpants. I need to get shot of it. I toss the dog-end on the floor.

'You wanna give me a hand?' he asks. 'We'll need to dry it off.'

'Alright,' I say.

'Cheers. Afterwards—I'll buy you an ice cream. We can talk.'

I nod. Because I'm hot, and hungry. I'll not tell him that I've never had a boy buy me an ice cream before. He might reckon that's pretty stupid.

The grass beneath our arses is sun-warmed. I've kicked off my trainers. Don't reckon my feet stink. We're sat face to face. Tackling the situation. My chocolate ice cream is melting fast. Pooling in the dent between my thumb and forefinger. I make slurping noises sucking it clean. Pete is having a similar vanilla problem. His chin is messed up with the stuff. We must look like idiots. Halfway through we swap flavours. His idea. Gives me a hard-on that's not easy to hide.

Here in the Walks, half shaded, half not, he wants to know why I lied to him that morning at the church.

'Dunno,' I say, wiping my sticky hands on the sides of

my shorts. I slip my t-shirt over my head, lay it on my lap, and put my back against the ground. 'You should try this.'

Pete unbuttons his shirt. Wriggles out of it. His chest is messed up with sandy-coloured hair that gets thicker around his belly button, before disappearing beneath the waistband of his black trousers. They're a little bit too small for him, muscle ruining the iron line. He's down on the grass alongside me, our faces watching each other. I can smell ice cream on his breath.

'Well—why'd you tell me your name was Tim Fysh?' he asks.

He thinks I'm a loser. 'Heatstroke.'

His laughter is deep. Amusement flooding his eyes. I don't hate either. Lift my arse far enough off the grass to get at the photograph, and hand it to him. 'This—'

Unfolding it carefully, he takes his time looking at the Fysh brothers, their eyes full of trouble. Maybe he's trying to decide what they're laughing about too. 'Figured you were here about Doug Fysh—fucking terrible thing.'

He'll never know the half of it. I can't believe it myself. Doug dead. And the Soldier in prison. Suddenly, all I can think about is what'll happen to Birdee's red boat. Who'll love it now? 'Give it back,' I say, holding out my hand for the photograph. This was a mistake. I should go.

'Steady on,' Pete says.

And I close my eyes. Though sunlight through the leaves, flickering here and there, leaks beneath my eyelids. 'Sorry,' I say.

'No worries.' Pete pushes on. 'Guess you and Doug were great mates?'

It hurts to nod.

'You pretending to be his brother, and all.'

'I guess.'

'How about Tim Fysh, you friendly with him, too?'

'Nah, hardly at all.'

'You don't have to lie. Small town, Joe. I was at Tim Fysh's funeral.'

Now I'm mad. Because I feel like a fool. 'Then why'd you ask if you already know?'

'Just talking.' Big smile all over his face. A pleasing gap between his two front teeth. 'It's a nice thing you're doing. You want me to put this in with Doug, right?'

'It's what Fysh'd want,' I say. 'Fysh and me were—'

Pete interrupts me. 'I'll do it,' he says.

'Alright.' Because he bought me ice cream, I owe him something more. 'It's easier to lie sometimes. That's all. I don't mean anything by it.'

'Okay.' Like it really could be.

Not far from this patch we're sprawled on are the toilets I fucked Hold-Your-Horses in. It'd be so easy to walk him over there. Offer my arsehole up to him. But I don't. Instead, he wants to know easy things. Like what was it like growing up beside the river with Birdee. And stupid things, like how far can I swim underwater on a single breath? 'Further than you, I bet.'

'We'll see,' he says.

And I ache for Birdee, who could swim the length of the lido beneath the cool surface on a single gulp of air.

'You okay?'

'I'm alright.' If I stay here with him, too much rubbish

216

will spill out of me. And he'll see the gaps. Big and impossible holes to navigate around. Places better filled up with insects buzzing, clever lies. I can't tell him about my whale. Birdee. And Fysh. Am I betraying him, lying here with Pete and his chocolate breath? 'Should go now.'

'Already?'

'Reckon so.'

He's buttoning back up his shirt. Sweat patches on blue cotton. But I can't smell his armpits from here. Must be the soap he uses. I watch him put back on his shoes and socks, tying his laces by memory. 'There's a film on—at the Majestic, Friday night.'

Pilot cinema's been boarded up for years. Never been to the Majestic, two towns over. 'What about?'

'Er—'

He's no fucking idea. 'You've no clue?'

'I don't,' he says. 'But—you'll come?'

I nod.

'Should I come pick you up?'

'Nah. Will meet you there.'

'Okay—see you Friday.'

'Alright—' He knows I'm not going to be there. And I'm relieved he lets me leave with one last lie.

The houseboat, abandoned, seems sad without the Soldier. Hard to believe I stayed here for a time. Not so much happy as content. Being here was living another life, like I'd been born to different people. A woman who wasn't sad. A man who didn't hate me. For a while I understood what it meant to be really wild. Rootless.

Everything's fucked up inside. I want to imagine a bunch of lads hiked out here to get stoned, necking beer cans under the big black sky. But that's not the truth. I can see where the Soldier's been. The way he's torn the shelf from the wall, scattering his books. Even the window is fractured in the shape of his fist. Makes me certain I should have come here, instead of home to the house at the Point. Yet I didn't.

Outside, roped to the dock, is Birdee's red boat. It's why I'm here. What I've come for. When I pull the cord, the outboard catches first time. Tide's full. Like I knew it would be. The creek beneath the boat is clear and sky-coloured. More still than I ever remember. Like this is the first time anyone, anywhere, has ever moved across this piece of water.

Doesn't take long to reach the mouth of the creek, where it opens into the river proper. Wet's fast here. I let the outboard die, chucking the marsh into a sudden silence. Jump out of the boat and onto the grass. Rope held tightly in my hand, all the while the tide tugging against us. Maybe the river wants us both?

Before, when I'd decided what to do with Birdee's red boat, I'd imagined something big to say. Because there's so much we're filled with. But nothing wants to come out of my mouth. So I just release my grip on the rope. And let go.

The river. Eventually everything collects on the surface, where it pools, and you can't help but take notice. 'How did we get here?' Dora says. She's big. Busting with the life inside of her. Even her hands look unfamiliar.

Fifteen miles from there to here. 'Dunno,' I say. Because I don't.

I've dragged the armchair from the living room outside. Stood it on the riverbank, facing the water. The old man says we look like gypsies sat out there, drinking. Fuck him. It's cooler here at this time. And there's nobody to care anyway. He's been all over my back like sunburn. Doing his best to drive me from the house at the Point, back out to the Soldier's place. Has a mind that I should live on the houseboat. I don't tell him that I've been out there already. That there's nothing for me.

But Dora and me. The two of us are like magnets. Same pole. Forcing each other away, no matter how hard we struggle to get close. Been this way since the *Ann Marie*.

Dora waiting at the back door. Big-eyed. Seen the fishing trawler pass by that afternoon. Asking me if it was over. Done. Me telling her Doug is here in town, beaten but alive. Not beneath the wet in some forgotten place past the Outer Roads. Saying she should fucking thank me that her baby won't be born in prison. That I can't understand how she'd be a part of it.

But this isn't entirely true. Because we've been at odds since she jammed herself between me and Fysh. Two stupid lads mucking about on the riverbank. Swapping spit and cum. Her, no way of knowing what she was getting herself into. From there to here—I don't reckon I can measure the distance in miles, or anything as simple. How do you measure these happenings. In tides? Water washing over us.

'Why'd you go marry Fysh if you knew what he was?' I ask.

'Why's anyone do anything?'

That's a stupid thing to say. I fold my arms across my chest.

'You already know why,' she says. 'Was the same for you.'

She's not wrong. The whole truth laid out bare. Sometimes you want something so badly, nothing can be done about it. That's how it was with Fysh. Like a fucking magician, he could conjure anything, in anyone. Even the tides. But it doesn't really matter what me and Dora believe. In the end, Fysh was just the lad we belonged to. 'You're right,' I say. 'Guess I do.' Legs stretched out before me, my palms stink of green weeds. I relax my arms, go back to the empty beer can I've been rolling in the grass.

Dora leans forward a little, her jaw ajar. It's something

Birdee would do. Makes me wish things between us were different. 'I'm not sorry Doug's dead,' she says.

'He was a cunt. But he didn't kill Birdee.'

'But I am sorry about Birdee's Soldier.' She glances over at me.

Still hurts like hell. Reckon it will for a while yet. 'Thought he'd come around. Get used to the idea that Doug didn't kill Birdee. Didn't plan on the Greenland—'

'How could you?'

'Fucking waste.' He squandered his life.

'How much—do you think is my doing?'

'Dunno?' It'd be kinder to tell her none of it. But I won't lie any more.

'I want to know.'

'Could ask myself the same thing.' I've thought about it plenty. Considered if they'd be alive if I'd never come back here.

'Wish I'd never met Doug.'

Rolling my shoulders in the cool breeze. 'If wishes were horses.' Seeing that the light on the water is something else. Falling in a way that I can watch the tide travelling the sur-face of the river, bright sliding this way and that, concealing what's beneath.

Wet cheeks and snot on her top lip, Dora says, 'You think we'll ever be over Fysh?'

'Don't ever want to be.'

She wipes the mess from her face. Red eyes. Her hand drawing small circles on her belly. 'You know I have to leave. Soon—before the baby's born.'

'My old man won't be happy about it.'

221

'I can't stay here.'

'You have the money—from Birdee's boat.'

Dora nods.

I've not told her what I've done with the boat. Don't reckon I will either. 'Where you gonna go?'

'Ouch,' Dora complains, the baby kicking again.

We walk back towards the house, her looping her arm through mine.

Big moon looking through the open window, watching what I'm up to. I'm sat on the end of the bed, sniffing the air. I reckon it won't be long before my nose is rammed with the stink of sugar beet, blowing in from the factory over the river, five miles out.

Dora's running around in my head. Way she peels back misplaced memories, like a wood plane stripping paint. Has me considering why all the women in my life disappear. These women are the bends in the river, the curve of the moon; they smooth me. Without them I'd be a hard line. Nothing left to do but tell the moon everything I can't say to Dora. Birdee. My mum.

Moon soothes me until I'm more alright than not.

I leave Dora at the bus station. Standing heavy beside her blue suitcase. Waiting. Because I'm thirsty, I decide to drop into the Bus Cafe for a cold drink. Maybe it's more than I'm telling myself. That my mouth is full with all the things I didn't say to Dora? And really, I need to dislodge the lump in my throat. Fucking regret.

Some lad I haven't seen before takes my order. 'Nah,'

nothing to eat. Brings back a can, pulls the tab for me. 'Don't bother with a glass,' I say. From this window I can see townies starting to board. The fat driver goes around the side with Dora's blue suitcase, comes back sweating. I take a swig from my can. She's disappeared onto the bus. Gone. Like a magic trick. I don't want what's left of my drink. Pay at the counter, and duck into the toilet for a piss.

Standing in here by myself, I reckon I look a bit messed up. Mirror says my dark hair needs washing. Curls coming mean I'm due a haircut. Armpits somewhere between alright and not. But my teeth are bright against summer skin, and my breath smells of nothing more than orange.

I leave the Bus Cafe walking out into the bright sunlight busting all over the place. Busy wondering if Pete will bother turning up.

'Joe—'

'Jesus fucking Christ,' I say. Somehow, Dora looks more pregnant than she did fifteen minutes ago. 'You've missed the bus, then?'

'Looks like it,' Dora says.

'What the fuck are you doing?'

'Was thinking—'

'About what?'

'The houseboat—' she says.

'You can't live out there—with a baby.' Wondering if she's gone simple in the heat.

'Who fucking says so?'

Fuck. Afterwards, maybe. When the baby's born. 'Why'd you wanna live all the way out there—on your own?'

'I won't be on my own.'

223

My old man will fucking kill me. 'Alright,' I say. Because she's right. Dora won't be alone.

'You good to drive?'

Dora nods.

'Come on.' And we walk back to where I've parked the Mini. Me hauling her heavy suitcase.

Pete is wearing a yellow t-shirt that makes his skin look nice. It's too tight, and I know it'll smell good. He's treading back and forth, behind three big arches. He appears, then he's gone, agitating me. Hasn't seen me yet. But it's too late to turn around. Can't go home. Dora's taken the Mini.

Got my hands stuffed in the pockets of my shorts. 'Pete—' I holler.

His head snaps up. Cheeks flushed. Hair gelled hard. My bollocks don't ache. But for a beat I am on the quay, calling him by another name.

Pete jogs down the stone steps, comes on over. We must look like two idiots standing grinning. Pair of twats not knowing what to say for ages. 'Didn't think you'd turn up,' he says.

Almost didn't. 'Here I am,' I say.

'Film's started.'

'Fuck—sorry.'

'No worries. We could do something different?'

'Alright—'

Snow on the ground is coloured purple in the first light. Water around the wooden jetty frozen. I'll have to take a pole to it. The brutal weather is keeping all but the hardest townies away from the crossing. Since I'm the ferryman now, a slow day means I'll be into a second packet of cigarettes before my shift ends. From here I can see down the metallic line, factories either side, chucking out rows and rows of rubbish. Messing up the raw blanket of snow laid out overnight. The bravest fishing trawlers are leaving the fleet, past the house at the Point, heading for Blackguard Sand on the Outer Roads. And I am reminded why I stay.

'Here,' Pete says, passing me a pole.

Up close there's a clear droplet of snot on the tip of his nose that reminds me of pre-cum. 'Fucking freezing,' I say, and we set about smashing the ice. Puzzled by the river. The way it stands stone-still here, yet restless over there. Doesn't take long, working hard to keep warm. Further down the jetty, Pete has cleared the ice around our boat. It's not much to look at. Bought it with the money Dora had no need for. He's loading two big bags, rammed with supplies for Dora and the baby. He treads back over to me. Stands rocking like a toilet chain, one black boot to the other. His breath smells of burnt toast when he grazes his bottom lip against my top. 'You still driving over to your old man's later?'

I nod. We're interrupted by old-woman noises. Moving me to purpose. I offer up my arm. She swats it away, says, 'I'd sooner fuckin' crawl.' Her name is Alma. She goes and comes every day, talking to me like I'm a cunt. Because of this, I like her.

With Alma on the ferry, I call over to Pete, 'Tell Dora I'll be over—day after tomorrow,' and I watch him move down the river on his way to the houseboat, hunkered down in the middle of the marsh.

My old man's complaining that he hasn't seen me in a while. Wish he'd make his fucking mind up. Seems to me that when I'm here, he'd rather I'd not be. I tell him I've been busy with work. But it's half the truth. He'd hardly want to hear about Pete. Or the Soldier. Drove across country to see him in prison. But he wouldn't talk to me. Guard there reckons it's normal early on. That he'll come around. He's wrong. And I have to swallow it whole.

I hang my coat on the back of the chair. Sit down across from him at the kitchen table. 'How you feeling?'

'Snow needs shovelling,' he says.

He'll never fucking change. 'I'll do it later.'

'Make sure you do.'

'Alright.'

'You seen Dora and the baby?'

'Last week.' I know he walks way out there when he can. He blames me for letting her live on the houseboat. Said she should stay with him at the Point. Reckons I've cheated him out of something. He's wrong. I don't tell him that me and Pete take turns hauling stuff out to her in the boat we bought. Because he won't see what he doesn't want to. Like Dora, this woman who is braver than anyone I know. 'You eaten?' I ask him.

Shakes his head.

'Want anything special?'

'What do I care?'

I get up. Take two tins of chicken soup from the cupboard. Pull the tin opener out of the drawer. Start warming soup in the saucepan. 'She'll be alright' I say. Because it's the truth.

After we've eaten, I get the shovel from the shed. Prop the back door open with one of the old man's boots. The kitchen throws a big block of yellowed light onto the path. Makes it halfway to the gate. I work quickly, liking the shovel noises, scuffing the stone beneath the ice. Sky's tar black and everywhere. Bloody cold, too. More snow's on the way. Soon enough the path'll be gone, disappeared again.

Pete is back to front. Does things differently. I'm kneeling on the rug wearing only my underpants and one white sock, trying to wrestle him out of his jumper. After his head emerges, his hair is taller than it was before. Face flushed, and his bottom lip chewed red. I tug at his trousers, his dick half-hard behind the zip.

'Hold on—' he says, hands massaging the muscles on my shoulders, last of the summer colour fading fast.

He's reading me. This is something I've not known before him. 'I'm alright' I say.

'Come here.'

We leave the floor behind. On the couch I put my head on his lap. Can still taste his tongue on the roof of my mouth. He reaches round for the paperback, it's brown and fucked up, but smells like childhood on the marsh. And he reads to me. He does this when I'm troubled. When I'm restless and wondering what the fuck I'm doing here, watching our underpants drying on the clothes horse. His words shape sounds that are strange and unfamiliar to me. But beneath the lull I hear Birdee and Fysh, and the wet running. The distance between us is the river.

Pete's snoring. And I can't sleep. The sofa is too small for the two of us, squashed up somewhere between fucking and his clever book. Uneasiness is stalking me again. I should reach behind my head and put out the light. Instead, I trace the lamp light. Dim to dark. Until at the edges it's so black I'm not certain I'm even awake. In this in-between place they appear at their brightest. Together in Birdee's red boat on the indigo line. Fysh bare-chested and rowing. His hair burning like a firework. Birdee singing a song I can't quite hear. No matter how hard I lean in. I'm alright. My dead are watching over me.

'What's wrong?' Pete asks, stretching like a rubber band.

'Nothing.'

He pulls me to himself. 'Go to sleep—'

'Alright.'
'You're not sleeping.'
'Stop fucking talking—'

Morning. I'm cold. Pete's book is jammed beneath my arse. He has one heavy arm across my chest. I manage to move without waking him. I find my t-shirt balled up on the floor. Put it on. In the toilet I piss for ages. Don't bother flushing.

From the kitchen I can see the fairground lorries sneak into town. I open the window and lean out for a better look, wind grazing my cheeks. Further out there's the familiar line. The tide is on the ebb, returning to the Outer Roads. From here the water looks like a river of glass.

Acknowledgements

Thanks to: Anne Meadows and Jonathan Lee for seeing something in my writing early on. Aki Schilz and the brilliant *Free Reads* scheme. Chris Gribble at the National Centre for Writing. Anjali Joseph who I had the privilege of being mentored by on the *Escalator* scheme.

My heartfelt thanks to Sarah and Kate Beal, Abi Fellows, Salma Begum and Matt Bates without whom *The Whale Tattoo* would be more an illusion than not.